CATS ON A POLE

Kano Press

Also by Betsy Robinson

Plan Z by Leslie Kove

The Last Will & Testament of Zelda McFigg

Girl Stories & Game Plays

*Conversations with Mom: An Aging Baby Boomer,
in Need of an Elder, Writes to Her Dead Mother*

CATS ON A POLE

a novel by Betsy Robinson

For man, time is a destroyer,
but for the Cosmos
it is an ever-turning wheel.
—The Hermetica

Row, row, row your boat,
Gently down the stream.
Merrily, merrily, merrily, merrily,
Life is but a dream.
—Anonymous

Chapter 1

WAR

"You think if you don't move, I won't kill you," murmured Joshua. "And don't pretend you don't understand me."

For twenty minutes, Joshua Gardner had been having a staring competition with the giant cockroach standing atop a precarious tower of cups, saucers, pots, pans, plates, and silverware in his kitchen sink. The bug flexed one of its hair-thin antennae, then froze. "You can't win," whispered Joshua. "The minute you're off the dishes, it's squish." The bug sipped scum-covered tea from the rim of a chipped blue plate and, rolling its prehistoric compound eyes and deducing with its thousands of superior photoreceptors that this hairy, harried, hoary, haggard excuse for a man was no threat, it emitted a puff of pheromones and breakfasted on stale toast. Joshua lunged, smashing the sink full of china as the bug skittered through the crack in the splashboard. "Damn!" he yelled clutching his bloody finger and kicking the metal utilities cabinet. "Damn! Damn! Shit!" he bellowed, having forgotten he was barefoot.

Joshua Gardner was having a crisis. It wasn't that George Bush had stolen the election. Joshua wasn't political. It wasn't that he hadn't been out of his Upper West Side apartment in a week. Nor was it the now-broken plates and cups in the kitchen sink, or even that his wife had left with the baby two weeks ago Tuesday and his girlfriend wasn't talking to him. Joshua was used to the ups and downs of life. No, this was another kind of crisis.

Joshua Gardner had a strong constitution: his body, mind, and spirit were a well-lubricated, perfectly synchronized system honed over years of practice. He had a fierce and virile heart that radiated warmth, and, even if they couldn't consciously feel his pheromone-packed emissions, women responded by falling in love with him. This had been happening all his life. "Love is sexual; there's no getting away from that," he told the ones who flocked to his healing classes. "Don't be afraid if you suddenly feel turned on." He grinned rakishly as he demonstrated laying-on-of-hands chakra healing, and the women blushed. Most of the men who attended his classes were gay. Occasionally there'd be a straight one who challenged his authority. Joshua couldn't help it if some people were intimidated by a strong leader; as soon as they realized there was no "winning," they'd leave. "When the student is ready, the teacher will come," he'd tell his female devotees as yet another frustrated male stormed out.

And now, sitting in his pajamas with two-day itchy stubble on his face, barricaded in his apartment by two weeks' worth of *New York Times* and no interest in current events, he wondered if it worked the other way as well.

The first time Harmony Rogers had walked into his school, it had knocked the breath right out of him, and Joshua Gardner was not one to be moved by appearances. "Is this the faith healing place?" she asked brazenly, and Joshua couldn't answer. She was small and dark, of indeterminate race— maybe half-Black, Italian, or some Semitic-rooted mix. She reminded him of someone famous, but he couldn't think who. Despite a bad haircut, she was pleasant looking, but nothing extraordinary. What was extraordinary were her colors—raw red and orange energy around her torso, a deep indigo, bluer than the bottom of the ocean with radiant purple wafting through it vibrating so fast above her head it made him feel faint just to watch it. But watch it he did. How could he not? Her desire was direct and raw. At first he'd tried to be sensible and professional: When he heard her think, "I wonder if he's married," he'd found a way to refer to his wife.

Poor Judy.

Joshua sucked his bloody finger and searched for a Band-Aid. He pulled organic cotton balls, Q-tips, rubbing alcohol, Witch Hazel, and natural laxatives out of the medicine cabinet. He overturned the hamper full of bathroom supplies and created a mountain of Tampax and super-size sanitary napkins. Damn Judy. Couldn't even leave him something useful.

He dug through his tool chest tossing strange size screwdrivers and hammers that he'd just had to own, nuts and nails of every diameter, hardware to long-discarded household appliances all over the kitchen, and finally he found the Superglue. Carefully, he coated the gash on his right pointer finger, then sat in the middle of the kitchen floor pondering what to do.

The answering machine took twelve calls from clients wanting private healing appointments. Mid-afternoon, Joshua decided he would try to shave. He had lathered his face and was contemplating a first razor stroke when the zap came. "Damn!" he screamed, arching backward, cutting the side of his cheek. "Damn! Damn! Damn!" he moaned as an erection took over and he hobbled back to the bedroom. "Damn," he sighed as warmth streamed up from his crotch, rivulets of excitement coursing through his body. "Damn!" he gasped after he came. The woman was driving him insane.

***

I'm evil, thought Harmony Rogers, stretching with pleasure after her orgasm and gazing around her Lower Eastside apartment. She breathed in Joshua's pungent smell—incense laced with a masculine bite—and she smiled, knowing that he couldn't resist her, but would never say anything. To admit to their energetic lovemaking would mean to admit to every sneaky seductive thing he'd ever gotten away with. After all, everyone knew he never touched his students, so how could it be his fault that they all fell in love with him? But he'd met his match with Harmony. She grinned and gave him one last zap from her pelvis. Then she climbed out of bed, opened the curtains, and wondered what she should eat and how she should spend the rest of this lovely Sunday afternoon.

***

Joshua missed his baby.

Harmony missed somebody, but she didn't know who. It was like a deep ache in the middle of her hollow chest attached to no thought, no story.

Joshua missed his baby so deeply he felt it as a searing pain. He didn't miss his wife, and this was a problem. His baby's name was Emily, and when he held her soft little body and she rested her smooth, luminous face in the crook of his neck, he felt a peace he'd never imagined possible. For years he'd taught his students that they were perfect, that any belief in imperfection was an illusion, but it wasn't until he first held Emily that *he* knew this to be true. He missed her in his heart, his blood, his bones. He missed her so hard he thought it might kill him. The only relief was when Harmony intruded with her raw sexual energy, and for a few minutes he felt out-of-control, hot and insane with pleasure. But when it was over, he remembered Emily and how it was the distraction from Harmony that had caused Judy to pack up two weeks ago and leave him with no food, a week's worth of laundry, and a subscription to the *New York* blasted *Times*! Damn her. Damn his recalcitrant girlfriend. Damn all women!

***

Harmony adjusted the hot water and stepped into her shower. Ah, just right. She closed her eyes and arched, surrendering to the hot spray pounding her chest and enveloping her breasts. She turned and let it stream through her long brown hair, hot rivulets massaging her back and buttocks as she soaped up. She was reaching for the loofah when she saw the antenna quivering through the crack in the caulking. "Jeezus Christ!" she screamed, lunging through the shower curtain, flooding the floor with spray, soap, and dripping shampoo. "Shit! Shit! Damn!" she screamed, flailing at the terrified cockroach with the loofah. It stared at her in shock, then skittered back inside the wall. "Damn you to hell, Joshua Gardner!" yelled Harmony, battling shower spray to turn off the water.

And on the Upper West Side, Joshua doubled over, laughing so hard he nearly peed in his two-week-old pajamas.

This was war.

Chapter 2

IN THE BEGINNING

It had begun a year ago on a Monday morning.

"Work it! Get into it. Feel it burn. Just eight more—and four, and three, and two, and one. You did it!"

Harmony huffed and collapsed, a sweaty flaccid lump after her one-hour Kathy Smith aerobic video workout. She hurriedly showered and dressed in her light-wool navy suit, white silk blouse, and pearls. Then, suddenly overcome with a thought, she froze for five minutes in front of her apartment door, unable to turn the knob, causing her to be late to work at the Madison Avenue offices of *Your Garden Magazine*, which she privately referred to as "the Teflon tombs." Although she was bored to a barely contained scream, the work was minimal and mindless, the money was steady, and the benefits were good, so she'd stayed for five years as managing editor.

Saturated with dread and resentment, she stepped out of the elevator into the chrome-colored *Your Garden* reception enclave: chrome desk, four faded chrome-gray wingback waiting chairs separated by acrylic side tables set on a chrome-gray industrial carpet, surrounded by gray walls filled with chrome-framed *Your Garden* covers from 1961—the only color in sight. The room was overseen by a gray-haired receptionist with chrome-rimmed glasses who was always reading. "I'm sorry," said Harmony, but the receptionist did not look up.

"I'm sorry, so sorry I'm late," she called as she scurried down the corridor past the office of Joseph Timiani, editor-in-chief, who, three months into the year, was still processing his fears about Y2K and frequently too upset or too distracted or just too something to reply. Joseph was a skinny, prissy white man with a taste for over-priced three-piece suits, floral wallpaper, Hallmark card art, and clear nail polish, and he hated tardiness. "I promise I'll work five extra minutes at the end of the day," called Harmony, loud enough to be heard as she slipped into her dirty beige cubicle and yanked off her coat. She knew Joseph hated her addressing—and exposing—his pettiness with such a loud and exact apology; they both knew she could finish her whole day's work in a couple of hours, and the rest of the time was about looking busy in case someone from the business office dropped by.

"It's not a problem; just don't do it again," snarled Joseph through a thin-lipped grimace.

"I insist," boomed Harmony from her cubicle, knowing he was checking his watch right now to record how many minutes this apology was taking. "And again, I apologize."

She spent the morning rejecting slush pile essays about favorite rose bushes, took lunch from twelve to one, and trafficked manuscripts and read a novel until precisely five minutes past five. "Good-night," she called to Joseph on her way out, knowing he'd stayed late to make sure she put in her extra five minutes. But he pretended not to hear. When Joseph was uncomfortable, he didn't respond. Harmony had gotten used to it and didn't wait anymore. The other editors were just as silent—a bookish group of women who rarely left their offices. Harmony wondered how they came to work at a gardening magazine, since they kept only cut flowers in plain glass vases and seemed almost phobic about dirt. The secretaries were sedate and the business people incommunicative. Everyone at *Your Garden* communicated by email—even to the next cubicle. "Good-night, everyone," she called into the emptiness as she hurried past the receptionist desk into the elevator, and nobody answered.

Who cares? thought Harmony, who had been hired for her current position after three weeks as a temp with "above-average organizational skills," according to the *Your Garden* HR department, who found her ability to sort and traffic and make lists "very competent." She'd been so excited, believing she would write articles and become part a plant-loving community. But a year into the job and the resounding silence of the tomb, she decided that she really wasn't that fond of people after all. She liked plants. So it was fine. For a while. The one big drawback was that Joseph was the only male employee, he was gay, and although she had no interest in physical contact, it was now five years later and she hadn't met even one attractive, available straight man.

"When stuff is stuck, it stinks," she'd told her therapist, trying to describe the problem. "I'm stuck."

"What exactly do you mean by that?" Dr. Thompson had asked.

"The energy. My energy. When it's all stuck in a missile, it starts to stink. I stink. I know if I could get myself to meet someone, it would start to move, but I don't like bars or singles activities or people. Basically I don't like anything."

With a quizzical look, Dr. Thompson had told her the hour was up, and for next session, she should think about interests that could expose her to people she'd like.

And this morning, she'd suddenly realized she did like something: energy—the energy that stank so much when it didn't move. All her life she'd felt it, smelled it, dodged it, reveled in it. Kathy Smith, her video aerobics teacher, had great energy. The way she looked into the camera so sincerely and assured Harmony that she could do just eight more leg lifts made Harmony believe she really could—that she could have "nice" energy like this pretty blonde white woman, that even if she could never really be nice, maybe she could do good things with her energy. Energy—good or bad—it interested her—this was the epiphany that had set her back five minutes.

"Energy?" asked Dr. Thompson, trying to sound nonjudgmental, despite Harmony's lateness and lack of explanation. "Can you elaborate on that?"

"You know—the stuff people give off when they feel or think. Sometimes it's hot or cold. Sometimes it stabs or cuts or envelops you. Sometimes it stinks—like what I was talking about last session. It depends on the person and the situation. Kathy Smith probably smells lovely, even after a workout. Cancer, on the other hand, is stinky. I know that's not a thought or a feeling, but maybe it comes from a feeling. I'm not sure. All I do know is Cora, the secretary in the cubicle next to mine, has a tumor in her stomach, and I swear, I could use a gas mask."

Dr. Thompson took a long sip of iced tea. "This is very interesting," she said readjusting her skirt to cover her thick calves. "Can you tell me some more?"

Harmony was paying $120 a session and was beginning to get annoyed. She'd been seeing Dr. Thompson for eight months—since her dog died and her suicide inclination had been hijacked by a sudden and seemingly permanent state of arousal—a bizarre manifestation of grief? It was more physical than emotional—like there was a missile of energy between her legs, and if she didn't blast off, she would blow up, kill somebody, or go mad—which was why she'd been jumping up and down with Kathy Smith for eight months. This energy destroyed her ability to be depressed, which at least would have been more rational than relentless arousal with no true desire for companionship. She'd tried masturbation, but seconds after the orgasm, the missile would return. And eight months of therapy hadn't made it any better. She glared at Dr. Thompson and ground her teeth. "I'm glad you find this interesting. I've never really tried to explain it before, but energy most definitely has a smell. For instance, if somebody has a really strong thought—the way you did when I was five minutes late for my appointment tonight—it smells."

"Excuse me?" said Dr. Thompson recrossing her legs and willing her foot not to tap. She had thought this was just an anxiety disorder following the death of a pet, but perhaps she had been too hasty in her diagnosis.

Harmony half-closed her eyes and softened the front of her body to feel Dr. Thompson's discomfort level. Very high. But $120! "When I was late and didn't apologize or explain but just started talking, you were annoyed," said Harmony, staring steadily so she wouldn't miss the reaction.

Dr. Thompson sucked in breath. "You feel I was annoyed?" she queried on a measured exhale. "Why do you feel I was annoyed?"

"Because you thought, 'She's five minutes late and hasn't apologized. Another narcissist. Lord, I'm sick of this. Well, I'm not saying anything if she doesn't, and I'm ending the session on time. I wonder if she'll protest.'"

Dr. Thompson turned crimson and took several controlled breaths.

"And now you're wondering if I'm delusional and a good guesser, or if I can really hear you think which scares the shit out of you because this isn't in the DSM, and how on earth can you deal with it?"

Dr. Thompson spilled her tea, slowly rose from her chair, and said, "Please excuse me for a moment. I need a paper towel." Then she walked out of the room.

Harmony felt a little guilty for how much she was enjoying this, and she gazed around the room trying to pick up clues about Dr. Thompson's personal life.

Harmony was interested in people's backgrounds. She had so little information about her own. She had been adopted soon after birth and had no knowledge of her racial roots. She'd been asked so many times what she was that by the third grade she'd begun telling people her birth parents were a Native American medicine man and a Middle Eastern gypsy who'd met in jail after being arrested for fortune telling. She'd told the story so many times that she'd almost come to believe it. After all, she did feel different.

Her parents were Rosemary and Larry Rogers, two hard-working white Christians who married too late in life to conceive a biological child. Harmony had grown up loved and admired, if not understood. When she would answer her mother's unvoiced questions or tell her father he worried too much, her parents would simply hug her and tell her what a sensitive girl she was, but she shouldn't spend so much time indoors. She should make friends with the other children in their suburban development of box houses with rectilinear windows so identical that you could get lost. It was a lostness particular to small towns awash in people who smiled and said good-morning no matter how angry they were at their husbands or wives or annoying children. When Harmony asked why the minister at church always pretended to like people when he shook their hands good-bye, but his hand smelled like dirty socks and he really hated everybody, her parents told her she could stop going to church. And she did. No big deal.

Harmony made very good grades, which seemed to compensate for the fact that she had no friends. She was a devoted daughter and had nursed both parents to the end of their lives. After her mother died was the first time she contemplated ending things. She was sitting on a bench at the East 72nd Street entrance to Central Park trying to choose between a pill overdose and "falling off" the subway platform when a stray puppy of indeterminate pedigree had jumped into her lap. The puppy had no collar, so what could Harmony do but take her home and name her Delilah?

They'd lived together for eighteen years—the longest relationship besides her parents that Harmony had ever had. And when Delilah died in her sleep last August, Harmony lost her focus. Her energy lost its focus and was trying to make her insane. Although she badly wanted to join Delilah and her parents, the missile forbade it, and since she was well aware that forty-two was too young to die, she'd decided to give therapy a try.

Dr. Thompson walked stiffly into the room with a roll of paper towels and dabbed at the puddle of spilled tea.

"I'm sorry I made you uncomfortable," said Harmony after what seemed like an interminable silence. "I was late to work and I had to make up the time. It's been a long day, and I'm guess I'm cranky."

"You think I'm uncomfortable," began Dr. Thompson, and Harmony stood up.

"Can we stop this? Please! I'm paying you to help me, and this doesn't help. I don't think you're uncomfortable. I know it. I know that right now you're wondering how much time is left in the session because as soon as I walk out of here you're going to pour yourself a stiff drink. Then you'll call a colleague to try to make sense out of all this and put it in a box with a label so you can be assured you've done the right thing. I know that right now you're scared to death because you've never felt so exposed. You're trying to think of all the stray thoughts I might have heard, and you're even more scared because you're actually believing I can hear you think. So maybe *you're* crazy."

All the blood drained out of Dr. Thompson's face, and Harmony sat down.

"You're right," said Dr. Thompson finally. Her eyes were soft.

"Thank you," answered Harmony, sighing heavily.

"Now how can I help you?"

Harmony closed her eyes and swallowed. She had never told anybody about her secret language before.

Chapter 3

LEARNING TO HUG

It was the first big snowstorm of 1963, and Harmony looked like an exotic cherub bundled in her new powder-blue snowsuit with a halo of soft brown curls poking out from under the hood, framing her oval olive-skinned face with full dark lips and round chocolate eyes. She was rolling around the back seat of the station wagon while Mr. and Mrs. Rogers swayed together in the front in time to their rousing, laughing rendition of "Happy Birthday." Harmony was giggling and trying to make a clapping sound with her mittened five-year-old hands. Her frustration made her parents laugh even harder, which made Harmony laugh and exaggerate her frustration, spreading her hands as wide as she could and missing the clap altogether, which made her parents laugh so hard they cried, and that's when they hit an ice patch and crashed into the tree.

Larry Rogers had always loved to dance, and Harmony looked forward to their ritual every night when he put her to bed. "One last dance with Daddy," he'd say as he held her tight against his heart and waltzed her to bed, her short legs dangling as she hugged him around the neck.

After the accident, there were no more dances. Sometimes Harmony would sit in his lap as he wheeled his chair, and they'd pretend it was dancing, but deep in her heart Harmony knew it wasn't.

Mrs. Rogers fared better, only losing her hearing, sense of smell, and memory from the head injury.

Harmony survived without a scratch. A second before the crash, a gentle but commanding voice had ordered her to "hug"—a game her father had invented to prepare Harmony for the air raid drills they were practicing in the elementary school. "Hug" seemed much nicer than "Duck," and he wanted to her to be safe:

"Hug!" he would boom, and Harmony knew to curl into a ball, hugging her knees around her head. Then her father would pretend he couldn't find her. "Where's my little girl?" he would say despondently. "My little girl has disappeared. And what's this big ball doing here?"—which was Harmony's cue to explode open her body and yell, "Here I am!" and her father would pretend to be stunned and gasp, "How did you do that?"

"Hug!" commanded the voice a moment before the car crash, and Harmony had survived the impact. But it was hard. Her mother never remembered who Harmony was, and her father couldn't scoop her up in his strong arms and make her feel like everything would be all right.

This was when Harmony's secret language proved valuable. She would hear her mother wonder if she had remembered to feed the little girl breakfast. Harmony would feel her mother's confusion and terror—the sudden shot of adrenaline—and she would calmly smile and mime how full and satisfied she was by rubbing her tummy, then she'd blow her mother a kiss.

But sometimes she didn't know what to do with her secret language—like when her father suddenly felt hopeless and scared. Once when they were watching *Singing in the Rain* together, Harmony felt a hard wad fill his throat as he choked on tears, remembering how he used to pretend to be Gene Kelly leaping around the living room serenading Harmony and her mother. And all Harmony could do was pat his hand and ask him if he wanted a cookie. She knew her father didn't know she was hearing his thoughts. And he would have felt even worse if he knew she felt his heart break inside her own heart, as well as every drop of his sixty-year-old's loss with no idea in her eight-year-old brain how to make it better. She tried to respond to him in her secret language—sending him a hug and warm feelings—but he didn't speak energy.

Sometimes Harmony would wake in the middle of the night screaming. "What is it? Tell Daddy," pleaded her father. But how could Harmony tell him that it was him? Him and everybody else—from her third grade teacher with the pain in her chest where her breast had been cut off, to the girl in the last row whose father was hurting her at night, to the boy in gym class with the funny looking foot who pretended not to care when the teacher told him he could be the scorekeeper when they played kickball. When she was younger—in kindergarten—Harmony would erupt in screams whenever the feelings came, but she quickly learned that this would result in trips to the nurse's office, then pediatricians and doctors who asked strange questions while they pretended to enjoy kids' games, but really they just wanted to see how she acted. So she learned to swallow the screams. The only time she couldn't control it was when she was sleeping. "Please, please tell Daddy. I'll kiss it and make it stop hurting," begged her father. And his pain made Harmony want to die, so she pretended it was a tummy ache, and let him kiss it, tuck her in, and turn off the light. She spent the rest of the night chewing on the sheets whenever the pain would come. And with so many people hurting, it would always come.

Chapter 4

THOUGHT-TALKING

Two weeks after telling her secret, Harmony arrived at Dr. Thompson's determined to speak only the truth. "As I mentioned last session, I'm not interested in anything except my secret energy language, and I don't like anybody. My boss, Joseph, had testicular cancer last year and lost one. When he hired me, he promised I could work my way into a straight editing job, and for five years, all I've done is perpetual tidying while he's taken my ideas and assigned them to other people. So most of the time, I want to kick his one remaining ball. Also, he has very bad breath, and he stands too close when he wants something. I don't like people's smells. When they get too close to me on the street, I want to slug them. I have evil thoughts all the time. But I think if I could just get rid of the crotch missile, I'd feel better."

"That's very interesting," said Dr. Thompson. She was exhausted from trying not to think.

"You can think if you want," answered Harmony. "Of the two of us, I have the worse thoughts, so don't worry about it."

"Our session is almost over, but I would like to suggest one thing."

"Oh, I almost forgot," said Harmony fishing through her purse and pulling out a folded piece of paper. "I wrote my letter of resignation:

Dear Joseph,

I quit, you manipulative, dishonest, oblivious, hypocritical bastard!

It was beyond insulting when, yesterday, I pitched the story about houseplants that heal—with information from original sources and firsthand experience—and you then discussed assigning it to another writer, to be edited by you who have no experience whatsoever in this field.

Can you not see how insulting this is? Do you simply not care? I am more qualified than all of the editors put together to work on this material, and you treat me like a waitress.

God, how I hate you. I wish you much pain and all the humiliation I have felt working for you. Die, why don't you?

Sincerely yours,
Harmony Rogers

Harmony took a breath and re-folded the paper. "What do you think? Too strong?"

Dr. Thompson was at a loss, so she continued as if Harmony were a rational person. "I realize you're lonely, Harmony."

Harmony looked startled. "Excuse me? I'm horny, but I'm hardly lonely. I just don't like anybody."

Dr. Thompson looked at her with liquid eyes, and Harmony quashed an impulse to grab her coat and flee. "Don't worry," said Dr. Thompson, "our time is almost up. But I would like to make a suggestion."

"What's that?" asked Harmony. She hated assignments, but she'd demanded Dr. Thompson help, so she had to listen.

"I want you to do some research. I want you to find a place or people with whom you can share your secret language—the energy language."

"Yeah, but I have no idea—"

"That's why it's called research. I'll see you in two weeks." Dr. Thompson rose abruptly.

Harmony didn't particularly like Dr. Thompson, so she couldn't understand her sudden desire to hug her. And she left.

***

"Hone your psychic abilities," said the ad in *The Village Voice*.

"Reiki Master Luanne Carpenter invites you to her weekly classes to experience your true nature. Carpenter, a clairvoyant healer with over a decade of experience, trained with Peruvian shaman José Guillardo as well as a renowned Tibetan Buddhist Rinpoche and Native American medicine women of the Diné and Nez Percé tribes. Classes 5 PM Saturdays, $35 each. All welcome."

The only reason Harmony went was to demonstrate an effort to complete Dr. Thompson's assignment. She'd gotten an icky feeling when she'd read the ad; most group activities gave her an icky feeling, but she was trying to keep an open mind—plus, the address was Broome Street, not far from Harmony's apartment, so if she didn't like it, she could be home in time for the six o'clock news.

Walking up the filthy, uneven steps to the fourth-floor loft required an act of will, and she paused in front of the pile of shoes outside the open front door. Hmm, thought Harmony. Then she slipped out of her loafers and entered in socks.

"Greetings," said a massive woman with waist-length, gray braids and long jeweled earrings. "Just make yourself comfortable." With half-closed eyes, she inhaled as if tasting Harmony, then gestured down a dark corridor to a dimly lit room. Harmony nodded respectfully and tiptoed down the corridor.

It was a nice room with floor to ceiling windows on three sides and a dance studio floor. In the middle was a small circle of chairs occupied by men and women in loose, dark-colored exercise clothes, sitting with perfect posture, eyes closed.

Harmony wondered if they were all yogis and quietly lowered herself onto one of the two empty chairs. If she'd had windows like this with an unobstructed southern exposure, she'd be farming—banana and orange trees, roses, gardenias. But all the place had was a ratty hanging spider plant and a couple of *dracaenas* that could live in a closet. What a waste of light, thought Harmony. Then suddenly remembering why she was here, she clamped closed her mind and searched the group for other thought-talkers. No one seemed to have heard her. She looked for the massive woman—the teacher—and found her standing at the entrance, eyes closed, swaying almost imperceptibly, her man-size hands clasped over her heart. Harmony wondered if she was married and how much she weighed. Then she swallowed hard, expecting a thought reprimand. . . . Nothing. The woman looked like she was in a trance, and Harmony couldn't feel or hear anything from her, so she continued musing.

Spider plants were known for their air-cleaning ability. Harmony wondered if there would be bad smells once everybody started doing whatever they did here. She wondered if anybody was listening to her, so for fun she looked at the slender guy with the red beard sitting opposite her and purposely wondered if he would like to have sex. She wondered if she went over and asked, if he'd leave right now. We could be in my bed in ten minutes and just forget about all this psychic stuff, she thought excitedly. And you wouldn't have to call me afterwards because I really just want to relieve the pressure. You see, if I could relieve the pressure, I could stop therapy and tolerate my miserable job better. God, what I wouldn't do for a really good— And that's when he opened his eyes, looked directly at her, and yawned. Oh my god, thought Harmony. If she ran out right now, would she still have to pay the thirty-five dollars? And that's when Luanne Carpenter hit the gong.

"Jeezus Christ!" gasped Harmony as her chair and body turned spastic with the vibrations. The others slowly opened their eyes as if waking from a deep, delicious sleep.

"Welcome, everyone," murmured Luanne, sliding into the seat beside Harmony. "Simon, would you raise the lights please?"

And Harmony choked with relief as Simon, the slender man with the red beard, daintily rose and sashayed across the room to the dimmer switch.

"Thank you, everyone, for coming to what will be a powerful experience tonight," said Luanne. "Since we have two new people, I'd like us to introduce ourselves. I'm Luanne Carpenter." She smiled and clasped hands with Harmony and the woman on her other side, and the whole circle joined hands. Luanne's hand was shockingly cold, and Harmony held her breath. She hadn't had physical contact with another living being since Delilah died. "Ow," she squeaked as Luanne nearly broke her hand.

"Please introduce yourself, then squeeze your partner's hand," whispered Luanne, smiling benevolently.

Harmony noticed that Luanne's breath smelled very bad—like rubber burning—the same as Cora, the secretary with the stomach tumor. She wondered if Luanne was having chemotherapy too. "Harmony Rogers," said Harmony, then carefully squeezed the hand of the woman to her left.

The eight other people introduced themselves all the way around the circle back to Luanne, who let go of Harmony's hand and began gesticulating. As Harmony wiggled the blood back into her fingers, Luanne explained that tonight she'd be doing channeling—that all day she'd felt the presence of some powerful healing entities, and she'd like to now welcome them into their circle.

When she had entered the room, Harmony had noticed the white ghostly being hovering above the beaded curtain exit to the rest of the loft. Now she waited while it slowly stretched and grinned. She wondered who it was and what it would say now that Luanne was acknowledging it. She had learned from experience that it was best not to acknowledge such beings unless you want to hear what they have to say. But much to Harmony's surprise, Luanne closed her eyes, completely ignoring the being, scrunched her face into a silly, slit-eyed expression, and started talking in a terrible Japanese accent. "I see many beautifuh faces. Ah so. Sooo beautifuh. Gleetings, my fliends."

"Greetings," replied the class, and Harmony stared at her lap. Out of the corner of her eye, she saw the being blow her a kiss, and she squeezed her eyes shut.

"I see we have two new peoples here tonight," bubbled Luanne in her ridiculous accent. "On behalf of all of us, I want to say it is our honor to offer you healing. I sense there are questions. How can we be of service?"

Luanne stared first at Harmony who quickly crossed her arms to protect her hands, then at the other new person, a fifty-something, baggy-eyed woman with pock-marked chocolate skin who'd identified herself as Ruth Gabriel.

"My son disappeared five years ago on his way to school," said Ruth timidly. "I wonder if you could—"

Harmony felt her heart split like it did for the girl in the last row of her third grade class, and she thought if she didn't get out of here this minute, she would scream or kill Luanne for inviting this with no possible way of helping.

"This we cannot help you with," said Luanne in the Japanese accent, and

Harmony exhaled. "It is your boy's karma. We feel for you, but we cannot interfere."

Ruth Gabriel sobbed despairingly, and people on either side of her wrapped their arms around her.

Luanne explained that the boy was safe with God, and it isn't for us to understand why such things happen; we must just trust in a higher purpose. Harmony checked her watch. Only thirteen minutes had passed. She was going to die. And it was with that exact thought that the room and Luanne and the people turned fuzzy—like a kind of light reflection from something bigger.

"You expect too much," said the ghost being, popping into sharp focus.

Harmony growled, "Shut up," and blinked really hard to recover her proper vision.

"Excuse me?" said Luanne, surprised out of the Japanese accent.

Harmony, realizing she'd spoken out loud, coughed and apologized. "I'm sorry. So sorry. It's this cough. I just wish it would shut up." She coughed twice more, then motioned to Luanne that she was okay.

"Do you need some water?" asked Luanne.

"No. Go on. Sorry," said Harmony, slumping down in her chair.

"You need to see the whole truth," said the ghost, and Harmony glared at her socks and counted. She would count the seconds like she'd done in the fourth grade when the heat in her body got to be too much. It would start at the base of her spine and cook up her back until her whole body was shaking and on fire. She'd heard about people who self-immolate and were discovered as only a pile of ash on their rocking chairs, and she always expected that to happen to her. "You judge too harshly," continued the ghost. "She's doing her best to help people."

Luanne was talking in the accent again and telling Ruth Gabriel that she'd been the best mother the boy could have had, and she should let the rest be in God's hands. Then she turned to Harmony, who despite wishing otherwise, remained visible. "What?" said Harmony. "I'm afraid I didn't hear you."

"We want to know your question. We sense there is something that brought you here tonight," repeated Luanne, and Harmony tried to think of something to say. Luanne waited. And waited. As the class began to shift restlessly, and since the last thing Harmony wanted was to cause a scene, she finally blurted, "Do you have cancer?"—just to say something.

Luanne looked startled.

"I don't mean to pry," blundered Harmony, "It's just that I smelled the chemo, and I wonder if you do have it, if you could use some of the stuff you said in your ad to heal it." Not only was Harmony out of control, she was being mean, but she kept going. "One of the people at work has cancer, so if your Reiki medicine works, maybe you could help her too. We're not close friends, but I don't want her to die."

The ghost held its face in its hands. Luanne said she didn't discuss her personal business in class. Then she ordered Simon to lower the lights so they all could meditate for the remaining forty-five minutes.

When Harmony got home, just for the hell of it, she looked up Luanne's credentials on the Internet: You could become a Reiki master by taking several weekend workshops for $1,500 a pop, during which somebody who'd paid somebody else several thousand dollars would give you a magic transmission making you a healer. Luanne's shaman teacher had written a self-published book that he sold on his URL, and he lived in Sedona, Arizona, where he gave weekend workshops.

"I tried," Harmony told Dr. Thompson at her next session. "Really. I stayed for the whole hour and even tried to thought-talk, but nobody but the ghost answered."

"The ghost," said Dr. Thompson matter-of-factly. She'd had a session with her supervisor who'd advised her to remain open and nonjudgmental, and she'd thought she was prepared. "There was a ghost in the room?"

"Well, technically it may not have been a ghost. Sometimes they're people who have never been in bodies, so technically they aren't dead since they never were alive in our sense—like the voice that told me to hug before the car accident. He—it feels like a he—he, the voice, doesn't have a body, and I've never seen him. Some things are not people. But this being in the psychic place, it was a person. I'm not sure that it was a ghost, but I don't know what else to call it. It was very opinionated."

"You see ghosts?"

"Not that often," said Harmony, beginning to feel self-conscious. "Look, I know this is hard for you. Maybe this would work better if you could hear everything I say like it was a dream. Then you could do dream interpretation, and it would still be accurate, since the whole thing *is* a dream anyway."

Before going into private practice, Dr. Thompson had done market research, which was how she learned that what people are most interested in is themselves. Dr. Thompson had been working her way through graduate school as a focus group leader for advertising agencies at the time of this epiphany, fancying herself to be more altruistic than her groups because of her desire to help people, so her initial reaction was disgust. But gradually, she came to learn that her disgust was self-disgust—disgust that she fancied herself so superior to the masses. It took many years for her see that her arrogance was an indicator of just how unworthy she felt, that secretly feeling self-important when she helped people was merely an antidote to her belief in her own insignificance. And it took many more years, two broken marriages, and four miscarriages to forgive herself for this and to realize that the desire for self-importance—if used as an entry point—was the doorway to everything good.

Dr. Thompson genuinely liked Harmony, even though she was a narcissist of the first order. In fact, before Harmony walked in for her first session, Dr. Thompson had been thinking of retiring. Thirty years of wretched childhoods and unsatisfying relationships was enough to burn anyone out. "That's quite a talent—seeing ghosts," she responded. "You said the ghost was opinionated. What were its opinions?" She smiled, and suddenly Harmony felt comfortable.

"Something about my not seeing the whole truth, my expecting too much—I don't know—ghost shit."

"Do ghosts shit?" asked Dr. Thompson pleasantly.

"I like you, Dr. Thompson," said Harmony after a while.

"I like you too," said Dr. Thompson.

"But you're worried I might be insane."

"Just a little."

"Okay. As long as we're clear."

"We're almost out of time," said Dr. Thompson. "I'm wondering what that ghost meant about seeing the whole truth."

Harmony shrugged. She was having an uncomfortable impulse. She hadn't hugged anyone since Delilah. "Would it be all right if I hugged you?" she asked as she was getting ready to leave, and Dr. Thompson opened her arms. "Oh," cried Harmony. "Oh my god." And she ran out of the room, forgetting to do the hug.

Dr. Thompson straightened the slipcovers and poured herself a Scotch. Maybe she wouldn't retire just yet. Maybe she was worthy of this client.

Chapter 5

JOSHUA'S GAMES

A year before his crisis, Joshua Gardner had paused at the entrance to his new school space—a former print studio with huge industrial windows and a grainy pine floor that he'd just sanded. He'd gazed at Judy nursing their baby on the one piece of furniture—a faded-green beanbag chair in a pool of light on the other side of the room. Sensing him, Judy had glanced his way with an expression of vulnerability and love that made Joshua weak. He was unworthy.

"She's hungry," whispered Judy, her soft arms cradling Emily to her breast.

Joshua watched until he feared he might burst from the feelings; then he rolled the sander to the elevator. "I'll see you in a bit," he called. "It's due back at the rental place by three o'clock." As he waited, he perused the newly painted sheet rock. For three years, he'd been holding classes in borrowed living rooms. Who'd have thought he'd have his own school? His own wife and baby? He wished his mother knew. He hadn't seen Estelle—he'd taken to thinking of her by her first name—for five years. The last time was at his father's funeral, and the needy expression in her liquid eyes made him nauseous. He'd stayed long enough to get her settled in the nursing home; then he made an excuse about having to return to New York for work. Estelle's last words still burned: "I'm worried you'll end up like your father, the poor sonofabitch." Then she gave him that flirtatious, conspiratorial wink as if to say she and Joshua had a special bond in their mutual superiority. Lord, how he despised that woman. How he'd longed to push his wife and baby and new school in her face. But as usual, she'd managed to evade any confrontation by becoming senile.

Occasionally, Judy looked at him in the same needy way, and it gave him the willies. They'd married the year after his father's death, and his mother had never met her or her granddaughter. Judy didn't understand, but accepted the situation. She respected Joshua's special senses and followed his guidance. After all, she couldn't imagine a more loving father.

The hardware store where Joshua had rented the sander was next door to a dilapidated movie theater that showed revivals and strange independent films that interested only a handful of people, including Frederic Bologna, the eccentric owner of the building. It was Frederic who'd told Joshua about the vacant loft for his school and introduced him to his girlfriend.

Frederic was in his eighties and squinted at the world through yellow eyes and a perpetual cloud of cigarette smoke. He'd been sitting in his kitchen having his hair cut the first time they'd met. Joshua was there to do an estimate on an apartment renovation and had never intended to start an extra-marital affair. But Frederic's stylist was irresistible—strong, secure, independent—everything Judy was not.

Frederic insisted Joshua stay for coffee, and one thing had led to another. Frederic seemed to take paternal pleasure in Joshua's seductive powers—everything Joshua's father had disparaged. Frederic considered Joshua a young protégé, a friend, and put him on the comp list to see movies whenever he fancied. "Bring your girlfriend," he'd urged. "I know how it is."

Joshua glanced at the marquee listings as he was leaving the hardware store, and had a sudden urge to see a movie. Any movie. He considered calling his girlfriend to join him, but Judy expected him back right after returning the sander, so he went alone.

"Where were you?!" exclaimed Judy two hours later. "I thought something had happened. I was ready to call the cops, but I was afraid to leave the place unlocked, and you have the keys and the cell phone! What the hell happened? Are you all right?" Her face was flushed and she was gripping Emily so tightly the infant started to cry. "Oh god, I'm sorry, I'm sorry," said Judy as Joshua took the baby out of her arms. "Well?" hissed Judy. "Where were you?"

"I went to the movies," whispered Joshua, rocking Emily and stroking her face. "Will you please calm down?"

"The movies?" sputtered Judy. "The movies?!"

"I got directed," answered Joshua pointing to the sky, and he kissed Emily, who stopped crying, made a sucking sound, and fell asleep.

Judy was furious, but the sight of Joshua rocking their baby and his look of adoration threw her into confusion. "Damn!" she hissed, stamping her foot and pounding her thighs with clenched fists. "Damn you, Joshua. What the hell does that mean—you 'got directed'? You said you'd be right back."

Cradling Emily in one arm, Joshua squatted beside the beanbag chair and gently pushed into its center, making an indentation just the size of Emily's body, and laid her down in it. His fine hands worked the material into a protective ridge around their baby, pushing and gently molding as if he were working porcelain.

"'I got directed' is no excuse," said Judy, once he had finished.

Joshua stood, his soft eyes peering into her harsh ones. "You know I have to follow the impulses," he said moving closer, his warmth enveloping her. "Orders from headquarters." He pointed again to the heavens and pulled her into his hot body, pushing his thigh between her legs.

"Oh god, Joshua, you can't keep doing this to me," murmured Judy, desperately trying to hold on to her anger. "It's not fair." She could feel his energy shoot up between her legs to her womb, strong as a pole. They felt like one body, liquid and hot, held together by the pole. She couldn't move and she couldn't resist him. "Damn you," she whimpered as he lowered her onto the newly sanded pine floor. "Damn you."

Chapter 6

JOSHUA'S GIRLS

Joshua Gardner was always a flirt. By the time he was six he'd realized his effect on females. At first it was inadvertent. "Please can I have the bike with the red bell," he said to his mother, smiling so his eyes lit up like he was thinking of something really funny.

"Do you honestly, truly need that bike?" his mother replied, acting as if she didn't believe him.

"You are so pretty, Mommy," responded Joshua. "You are the prettiest mom of all the moms in my class. I honestly, truly mean that."

"Prettier than Pete's mother?" asked Estelle Gardner flirtatiously.

"Pete's mom?" gasped Joshua. "She's a dog compared to you. A real bow-wow. You're prettier than all the moms in the whole school! Honestly, truly!"

"Come give me a kiss then," said Estelle Gardner conspiratorially, and little Joshua would—acting like he was her boyfriend instead of her son because he knew she liked it and he honestly, truly wanted that bike.

Joshua never got along with his father. Joshua hated how his mother bossed his father around, but he hated his father worse for letting her do it.

"Make sure Norman's steak is well-done," Estelle Gardner would tell the waiter every time they went out for Sunday dinner. "He's squeamish." Then she'd wink at the waiter conspiratorially. Lord, how Joshua hated the name Estelle.

By the time Joshua was thirteen, he realized the power of his smile. He lost his virginity at fourteen, and by sixteen, had the record for the most girls having a crush on him in his grade. It was exciting to walk down the halls of Beale High School seeing them blush at his wink. It made him feel strong. Important. By the time he was eighteen, he had been in love approximately twenty-five times. But by the time he was dropping out of college, he wasn't so sure. Excitement, yes. Lust, god knows. But as soon as the girl returned it, it was as if something inside him died. And the longer he stayed with her, the deader he felt, until it became a kind of torture. He knew he was a bad person for going through girls like a guy on a shopping spree. He didn't intend to hurt them. He just loved a lot of women . . . for a short time each. Maybe this was just his fate. But if he really loved them, why did he feel so hollow after lovemaking? Why did his heart ache and his gut feel so sick?

He moved to New York City after dropping out of college. There, he worked on construction sites by day and painted at night. For a time, he was very depressed and drank a lot, but much to his amazement, that too attracted women. Beautiful women who longed to take care of him. They threw themselves at him wherever he went. "Who is this?" he'd wonder in the initial excitement of the first lingering look from a shy, but clearly interested, beauty who paused in front of his work site. The other men would stare lasciviously, but not Joshua. He'd smile sheepishly and apologize for his Neanderthal buddies, and before he knew it, he'd be in bed with the woman swearing this time it was the real thing. But in the morning, there'd been the emptiness along with the dread of weeks of phone calls followed by pleading notes, and finally an enraged diatribe—which he knew he deserved for once again being unable to feel even a drop of desire for this now-pathetic creature he'd briefly found so irresistible.

When he was forty-three, he met Judy. By then, construction work had taken second seat to massage therapy, where he discovered he had a gift.

He didn't understand how it worked; he just knew that when he touched people, his hands grew hot, his heart exploded, the room filled with colors, and sometimes helpers in subtle bodies would instruct him where to touch. And the clients felt better. Sometimes it was emotional, but sometimes tumors and diseases disappeared. Word spread and soon he had more clients than he could handle and turned down construction work, except for the occasional apartment renovation. By the time he met Frederic, he'd decided to open a school. He was just married and wanted to put down roots.

Judy worked as dental hygienist. She was pretty, warm, and maternal and never hurt his mouth. The subtle helpers told him she would be a good mother to his children. He loved Judy as much as he'd ever loved anyone, and he wanted children.

Frederic was a good friend. He knew how it was for men like them—they just couldn't conform to society's rules. When love presents itself, you have to say yes. And so Joshua had started the affair with the hair stylist.

Chapter 7

FINDING GRACE

Joseph Timiani was having a bad day. He liked being editor-in-chief of *Your Garden Magazine.* He liked being in charge. But he didn't like anybody knowing that he liked it. Or that he watched exactly how many minutes lunch break everyone took, or that he'd lied about having no choice in the decision to deny raises this year. He hated complimenting people because he didn't want anyone thinking they were too valuable. And he hated all this about himself because he knew if other people knew what a power-hungry, petty, conniving cheapskate he was, they wouldn't like him. And second to needing to be in charge, Joseph needed to be liked. When he wasn't, it hurt his feelings.

He was having a particularly bad day because Harmony Rogers seemed to know all this about him and clearly did not like him. And since she was a scrupulously well-organized managing editor with a photographic memory for all the details Joseph found so tedious, he couldn't fire her. Also, she fulfilled some minority or equal opportunity hiring requirement, although he had no idea if she was indeed a Black person with Asperger's since it was against his politically correct policy to ask about people's race or mental problems, and he would never give her grounds for a lawsuit by bringing up the subject. To cover his guilt and fury over the entire situation, he had bought her a *Brassolaeliocattleya Hermione's Dance* orchid and placed it on her desk this morning, and she hadn't said thank you! Not only that, but the woman was oblivious to the fact that he was her superior, which was his own damned fault because he went to great lengths to act like a regular guy—which made him even angrier. All of this had upset his ulcer, which was already inflamed due to the rejection by Quentin, his lover and the publisher of *Your Garden.* And even worse, he was in the toxic predicament of hiding his broken heart and all its ramifications because it was *his* policy to prohibit inter-office romances. What a stupid rule since, unless all the women were lesbians, he was the only one affected by it. This was all Harmony Rogers's fault.

It wasn't that she was flirtatious—no, not at all. Nor was it her appearance, which, if anything, lacked style; her hair was unforgivable. There was nothing you could pinpoint, but there was something about the air around her—Joseph couldn't say why, but it was terrifying. So just in case she hadn't picked up his preference for men, he thought it best to enforce sexual barriers via the ban on inter-office dating. Joseph was nearing retirement and he'd be damned if he'd have any sexual discomfort in his workplace. But she could at least acknowledge a seventy-five dollar orchid!

Harmony placed the new orchid out of the way on the windowsill. She had another priority. Two months ago, she had rescued a near-death *sanseveria* from somebody's garbage. It was a sad mess of bug-bitten snake leaves, dull from lack of sunlight, sticking up every which way. It's not easy to kill a snake plant, so somebody had willfully neglected this little guy to bring it to such a sorry state.

When she had removed it from its cracked plastic pot, the soil was so dry it scattered like dust. She had washed its six stiff leaves, gently scrubbing away years of grime, to expose a faint reminder of its yellow variegation. She had repotted it in fresh, wet soil in a heavy stoneware pot.

She shared a window with northern exposure with Cora, the secretary with the stomach tumor. Since Cora didn't have office plants, Harmony had appropriated the entire sill for her sick ward of rescuees.

Friday, Harmony had found the snake plant pushed halfway out of its pot and tipping into the anemic philodendron and the leggy rubber tree. She was so excited, she'd almost hugged Joseph. She wondered if that was the reason for the incredibly expensive, incredibly ugly orchid. Maybe he was trying to be a "regular guy" again. No matter. She could hardly wait to get on with the next stage of the snake plant's recovery. She spread newspaper on the floor, and sat down to repot it in an even heavier stoneware pot with appropriately decorative snakes carved around its circumference. She'd told Dr. Thompson about her rescuing houseplants hobby, and Dr. T had suggested she join a garden club—a great way to meet heterosexual men.

"Harmony, Joseph was looking for you," said Cora from the other side of their cubicle divider.

Harmony breathed through her mouth. "Thanks, Cora."

"He wants to see you right away," said Cora.

Harmony recoiled from the puff of thick, heavy, blood smell that blasted through the cubicle wall. The smell of anger on top of chemo was almost unbearable. "I'll go in a few minutes, Cora. I'm in the middle of something."

"He *is* your boss," said Cora, now standing at the entrance to Harmony's cubicle, arms akimbo, with her perfect blonde wig slightly askew atop her little head. "What are you doing?"

"I'm repotting a plant," answered Harmony, trying to mouth-breathe. Despite Cora's bossiness and bad smells, she didn't want to offend her.

"Oh," said Cora, eyeing the newspapers and soil. Then, rearranging the stapler, Scotch Tape dispenser, and paper clip holder on Harmony's desktop, she said, "He wants to see you right away."

"So you said," said Harmony, filling the new pot with soil from her special mix bag. "He can wait five minutes."

"People don't like it when you ignore them," said Cora.

Cora's smell was always worse right after a treatment. "I didn't mean to ignore you. I just—"

"Oh god, not me," said Cora, laughing at the absurdity of the idea. "Joseph. He's your boss, and it hurts his feelings when you don't respect him."

Harmony experienced the feeling of Cora's stomach tumor in her own body and was suddenly overcome with nausea. Good god, the thing was growing! She wanted to tell Cora she knew, and if there was anything she could do, please just tell her; that there really is no such thing as death so Cora shouldn't be afraid even though she was only thirty-four. And although Harmony could hardly keep from gagging on the stink of the chemo, she wanted to throw her arms around Cora and scream, "Don't die; please don't die." All this transpired in the second between Cora's last sentence and the next:

"You know, nobody likes a know-it-all. You should be more polite to your boss." Then she wheeled around, discharging a cloud of anger, and disappeared into her own cubicle.

***

"Thank you for the orchid, Joseph," said Harmony from the entrance to his office. "Cora said you wanted to see me?"

Joseph looked up from his copy proofing. He hated the way Harmony held back, forcing him to invite her in. "Yes, come in please."

Harmony tiptoed in with her arms tightly crossed. She knew how territorial Joseph was, so she tried to limit the amount of space she took up as well as her contact with the floor. "The orchid is lovely. Why did you give it to me?"

"It's secretary's day," answered Joseph, taken by surprise. Never a cordial preamble. The woman had no social skills.

Harmony sucked a deep breath. She'd had no intention of doing anything but repotting her snake plant and going through the day's submissions, but something snapped. "I'm not a secretary," she retorted.

Joseph's neck hairs prickled. "I'm aware of that. It was merely a gesture to keep you from feeling left out."

"Well, thank you for the gesture," said Harmony. And although she was willing her body to turn and walk out the door, her mouth had a different idea. "I didn't come right away because I was repotting that snake plant I found two weeks ago, which gave me an idea for a feature: 'Are You a Plant Rescuer? How to Make a Garden from Other People's Discards.' What do you think?"

Damn this woman. You never knew what was coming. "Well, that sounds like an interesting feature," answered Joseph, feeling completely unbalanced. "We'll have to consider it."

"If you decide to do it, I want to write it," announced Harmony, even though Joseph was emitting the sour smell that always portended something unpleasant. "I've been doing plant rescue for years and am something of an expert. In fact, if you decide you want the piece, I would like to do it as a full-fledged editor. I don't mind continuing to manage while you look for a new managing editor, but I feel like it's time I was promoted—as we discussed five years ago."

Damn it to hell. Joseph clenched his fists under his desk, and his face turned dark red. He'd given the woman a seventy-five dollar orchid, and this is how she responded! It took all his will power not to erupt in the tears and screams of a four-year-old. "Well, I certainly will give that some thought."

Although she knew she should say thank you and return to her cubicle, Harmony planted her feet so her soles practically sank into the pink floral carpeting, and she said, "You've been thinking about it for five years. I really would like to know when I'm going to become an editor here."

Joseph's complexion drained to an icy white, and his right eyelid twitched. He would not be bullied. Ever! "To tell you the truth, Harmony, the odds are not good. You are a very capable manager, but you lack the diplomacy required of an editor. I dislike these sorts of discussions, but since you've insisted, I must say the odds are not good."

"Oh," said Harmony. "Well, thanks for the orchid." And she left.

Joseph pursed his lips, and ignoring the fact that he'd forgotten to voice his bogus reason for demanding Harmony's presence—as well as the fact that she hadn't thought to ask—he sent an email to the senior editor: "I'd like to do a December feature on found plants—discarded houseplants brought back to life by the tender loving care of a windowsill gardener. It will be perfect for winter—bring the garden inside. See if that writer who did the piece on low-light office plants would be interested. Let me know when you've assigned it."

With her entire being, Harmony wanted to scream, "I quit, you slimy, one-balled bastard. You lying, petty control freak. You manipulative creep. I'm glad that sonofabitch Quentin broke your heart and your ulcer is burning, and who the hell are you to say I'm undiplomatic?!" But instead, she went back to her cubicle, sat on the floor, and finished repotting the snake plant. She'd just started enjoying therapy and she needed to keep her health insurance. Also, it's a little trickier to find a new job when you're in your forties.

"He gave me one too, you know," said Cora through the cubicle wall. "It looks like some kind of *bromeliad*."

"Those things die right after they flower," answered Harmony.

"I think it flowered a month ago." Cora was now standing at the cubicle's entrance, and although Harmony was facing the north wall, she could feel Cora's eyes drilling into her back. "So how'd it go with Joseph?" prattled Cora.

"I hate him," said Harmony, gathering the newspaper and plant scraps. "I forgot to ask him what he wanted, and he forgot to tell me. Happy secretary's day."

"That's kind of strong, don't you think?" said Cora, suppressing a smile. She loved it when Harmony got upset. Most of the time she was so arrogant. Then with a sudden feeling of guilt for her pleasure, she said, "Listen, I'm having an early dinner with Grace. Quentin gave her a complimentary meal for two at her favorite restaurant—the Chelsea Cove. Would you like to join us? We could split the third dinner."

The most satisfyingly predictable part of Joseph's behavior was his frantic attempts to make amends after he realized somebody was onto the fact that he'd screwed them. "Yes, I'd love to have dinner with you and Quentin's secretary. Isn't Quentin a wonderful man?" answered Harmony loudly as she felt Joseph exiting his office to come talk to her. "I heard he gave Grace a bonus for finding the new cover designer. Now that's integrity. He could have taken all the credit himself." She turned just enough to watch Joseph in her peripheral vision as he flinched, stopped, then disappeared like a well-dressed rodent back into his office. Gotcha, thought Harmony. Maybe he'd give her a guilt raise. And she got up off the floor, placed the plant on the sill, cleaned up potting scraps, and settled into her chair to begin the morning's rejections.

***

"Why did Grace pick such an out-of-the-way restaurant?" asked Harmony as she and Cora switched from the West Side cross-town to the downtown bus to Chelsea. "Doesn't she live on the Eastside too?"

"She likes it down there. It's near her school," answered Cora.

"Her school?"

"I don't understand exactly what it is. You can ask her yourself at dinner." Cora suddenly felt annoyed that she'd invited Harmony who asked questions in a way that made her uncomfortable. The woman must never have heard of small talk. Cora wondered if her wig was on straight. It was hard to know when it was under a scarf. The chemo was starting to hit her, and she hoped she'd make it through dinner without throwing up. She didn't even like Harmony, and she knew Grace had only invited her because she felt bad about the cancer. What had possessed Cora to invite Harmony?"

"I heard that Quentin finally met a girl," said Harmony, trying to make small talk. "Has he ever been married?"

"Rumor is he's gay," said Cora, settling into a window seat. She was glad they'd beat rush hour. "That's the only reason someone that good looking, his age—" and she stopped, remembering that Harmony was in her forties.

"Don't worry about it," said Harmony before she could stop herself. "I mean, I heard the gay rumor too."

Cora forced a smile, then turned to look out the window as the bus crept down Seventh Avenue. Harmony slouched in her seat and began to fantasize. First, she thought of an actor whose name she couldn't remember. He wasn't particularly good looking, and he never played the romantic lead, but every time Harmony saw him in a movie—no matter if he was a best friend or a drunk or a thug—she got the hot feeling. It was his eyes. Even if his character was an idiot, there was a knowing behind his limpid eyes, and Harmony thought if she could just meet somebody like that, they would look at each other, and without words, they'd both "know," sex would be incredible, and it wouldn't matter how much she hated her job.

Then she turned her gaze to the man sitting across the aisle, and for no reason in particular, she wondered if he was such a person. He had a nice body, but nothing special. His hair was dark brown and needed a cut. He had paint on his stone-washed jeans, and Harmony wondered if he was an artist. His eyes were closed, but she imagined they were blue. Blue like the ocean on a really clear day but still somehow soft—not piercing or cold but peering and gentle. His jacket was brown leather and worn at the elbows. She imagined he cared about his appearance but had cultivated nonchalance. And he was smart. Very smart. She liked that. His hands were folded in his lap, holding a pair of brown woolen gloves, and she was surprised by their fineness. She imagined holding hands with him, and as her pelvis flooded with warm energy, the man opened his eyes, pressed the signal button, then turned and winked at her. "They're green," he said. Harmony gasped. The man waved, then headed up the aisle and stepped off the bus.

"Oh my god," sputtered Harmony. "Oh my god."

"What's the matter?" asked Cora, pulling her gaze from the window and hoping the explanation wouldn't take too long. The next stop was theirs.

"Nothing," said Harmony, gulping air. "Nothing at all."

Grace had left work early for a doctor's appointment and was meeting them at the restaurant. "Hi. I hope you didn't have any trouble finding the place." She smiled at Harmony. "Glad you could make it."

"Me, too," said Harmony. Since they worked in different buildings, she only knew Grace from brief conversations at office parties. But there was something she'd always liked about her. Grace had a soft, warm quality, and she didn't wear make-up. For lack of a better way to express it, she looked "real." That's what people said when they mentioned Grace, and since she worked for the head guy, she got mentioned. Everybody liked Grace. She was easy to talk to.

"I like your hair," said Cora settling into the wall end of their booth. "Is that a new color?"

Grace looked at her softly. "No, I don't dye my hair."

"Oh," said Cora, suddenly busying herself with the menu. "Well, it's nice. What's everybody going to have?"

"Thank you," said Grace. "When I was a hair stylist, I always used to tell my clients who had chemo not to worry. Almost all of the time it comes back even stronger than before. I think I'll have the Portobello mushroom. What do both of you feel like? Think big. Quentin's paying for most of it." She winked at Harmony.

The Chelsea Cove had warm peach walls, distressed wooden tables with straw place mats, and felt like the singer Anne Murray singing *Old Cape Cod*—kind of slow, low, easy, and relaxed. Just the kind of place Grace would choose. In fact, it felt so much like Cape Cod, you could almost forget that right outside were honking taxicabs speeding down filthy, under-lit streets, dodging irate pedestrians who shook their fists as they crossed against the lights.

"I think I'll have the lobster," said Cora after a thorough perusal of the menu to determine the most expensive entrée.

Harmony chose organic ravioli and a garden salad, and Cora gave her a snide look for ordering cheap, which in Cora's mind made herself look greedy. Harmony wondered why she'd said yes to this dinner and if there was a way to cut it short. After all, she could be sitting home alone missing Delilah and masturbating. "So you used to be a hair stylist, Grace?"

"Yes," answered Grace.

Harmony tried to hear what was behind her smile, but there was nothing to hear. No thoughts. Just a smile. What to make of this?

"You can learn a lot cutting hair," said Grace, breaking a brown bun in half and coating it with butter. "For instance, you can always tell someone who cuts their own hair because they slice it sideways. The key is going with the grain." She took a big bite of bun and chewed, staring at Harmony. And the weird thing was that even though Harmony sometimes trimmed her own hair, she felt comfortable.

"Go with the flow," said Cora, breaking a bun also. "That's one of my stupid sister's favorite sayings. She's into crystals and that sort of thing. She told me my cancer is a *gift*. What a moron." She took a big bite of bun, followed by half a glass of water.

"I was a good hair stylist," said Grace. "But I developed Carpal Tunnel." She held up her right arm, crooked at the wrist. "Had to have surgery."

"Oh," said Harmony. "Is that what your doctor's appointment was about?" Cora shot her a horrified look, but before Harmony could descend into confusion, Grace saved her:

"No, it was gyno time. What a thrill!" Her face crinkled and she reeled with laughter. Cora and Harmony caught it and laughed too.

Harmony hoped she hadn't offended Grace, and tried hard to hear any unspoken thoughts, but still there was nothing. How peculiar. But it felt good to laugh.

"So Cora tells me you're going to school," she said in the next lull, hoping this wasn't intrusive. "What kind of school? Are you changing careers again?"

"Actually, I graduated a couple of years ago, and now I work there on weekends. It's a healing school."

Oh my god, thought Harmony, finally hearing some thoughts. She was dying of curiosity, but she sensed she should be very careful. "What's a healing school?" she asked nonchalantly.

"Would you like to hear today's specials?" asked the waitress, and Harmony wanted to slug her.

"No thanks," answered Grace cordially. "We're ready. And by the way, we'll be paying for part of the tab with a gift certificate."

The three women ordered, and the waitress left.

"So you were saying—about your school?" said Harmony, trying not to sound too eager.

"It's kind of hard to explain," said Grace slowly. "It has to do with energy—using it to know yourself better."

Cora snorted, and Harmony drained her water glass.

Chapter 8

JOSHUA IN DREAMLAND

Maybe it was bad ravioli, or maybe something else, but Harmony tossed and turned. Finally, at two a.m., she got up and ate a dish of vanilla ice cream while watching escort service commercials on channel thirty-five. How many men were sitting in darkened rooms all over the city watching these naked women, and how many of them would actually order someone to come to their apartment and have sex? If only there'd be a commercial of a man insane with desire for a woman so she could relieve her own tension, but after the naked women came naked men, and then people labeled "shemales" with breasts and penises. Harmony turned off the television and ate grapes. At three, she went back to bed.

It had been such a bad night of insomnia that when she first saw the man with the green eyes and the fine hands, she wasn't sure it was a dream. She was walking Delilah in the park when he approached. "Hello?" she asked tentatively. "Don't I know you?" But he didn't answer. He just softly yet easily penetrated her with his glittering green eyes. She felt him examining her—traveling down inside her body, lingering here, nudging her there. And at each linger and nudge, her body released until she felt boneless and muscle-less, a seething caldron of sexual energy. "Who are you?" she asked, but instead of answering, he spread his arms so his fine hands were on either side, as if energetically embracing her. His warmth spread through her like the softness you feel when you're dead tired and drop your heavy head onto the finest feather pillow and sink in. No tension. Just tenderness. And she drifted into deep sleep.

"Delilah?" she called, as the alarm buzzed and she woke with a jolt. Then she remembered. And cried.

It was like this every morning. Her neighbors had asked if she was going to get another dog, as if Delilah were a replaceable piece of furniture. When she answered no, they said, how about a cat?

Harmony thought about cats as she rolled out of bed and staggered to the bathroom. Her favorite cat was the one that used to get stuck on top of a telephone pole in front of the house where she grew up. At least once a month in the warm weather, she'd hear the neighbor kids yelling, "Cat's on a pole!" as they gathered around to taunt the poor thing.

Harmony would watch the scene from her kitchen window, and a couple of times she tried to thought-talk the cat down. "Are you out of your mind?" the cat would answer. "They'll kill me."

Once Harmony asked the other kids to leave the cat alone because they were scaring him, but they laughed and from then on, called her Crazy Cat Girl. So after that, whenever she heard the crowd gathering, she'd hide in her closet until one of the parents called the fire department. Once, after the firemen had come and gone and the circus was over, she asked the cat why he kept climbing up the pole. At first he pretended not to understand her; then finally, flicking his tail and walking away, he answered, "To look down on them all."

No, she would not get another pet. She missed Delilah. She cried. She washed. She got dressed and went to work.

***

Dear Harmony,

I have given some thought to your rescued plants pitch. I think it's a good idea. However, it's my best judgment that we assign it to an experienced writer. Thank you for your good ideas and exceptional management skills.

I will be taking the day off for my annual colonoscopy, but I trust you have everything under control. If you would like to take Cora to lunch for her birthday, please feel free to charge it to my account in the cafeteria. You can code it professional entertainment.

All the best,
Joseph Timiani

Joseph had used the snake plant as a paperweight and someone—probably the night cleaning staff—had knocked it over, breaking two of the leaves. As Harmony brushed the broken leaves and bits of soil into the waste basket, she began to cry—first, because of her maimed plant; then because she hated her job and missed Delilah; and finally, just because. She didn't make any noise. She'd learned the art of silent crying long ago. She missed her father. She missed how he would touch her gently and ask where it hurt. She missed somebody—anybody—who could "hear" what had no words.

"Harmony, are you all right?" It was Cora.

"Sure, I'm fine. Happy birthday," answered Harmony, busying herself with some papers.

"Thanks," said Cora, surprised that Harmony remembered. "Grace asked me to tell you that that school she works at is having an open house tonight. She wondered—"

"What time?" barked Harmony, "and do you have the address?"

***

The walk from the subway had been dark, and there'd been no sign for the school on the old industrial building's directory in the lobby. Harmony had pushed every button on the elevator, and only the sixth floor opened.

As she stepped out of the elevator, she glanced around the reception area. "Is this the faith healing place?" she asked at the desk. "Is Grace here? I'm sorry, I just forgot her last name. I'm bad with names when I'm excited. I wish I had done my aerobics this morning. Kathy Smith—have you heard of her? An excellent teacher. Very calming. Grace said there was an open house."

As a healer-in-training, the receptionist knew it was her job to be helpful and compassionate—even if this strange, intense person was an hour early. "This is the—," she began, but was interrupted by the creak and rattle of the freight elevator. The doors clanked opened, and the receptionist smiled adoringly.

"Huh?" said Harmony, turning to see who it was, and, my god, it was him—the man from the bus. "Is this the faith healing place?" she asked him, and she watched his discomfort as he recognized her.

"You visited me last night," she thought-talked. "I was walking my dog, and you came. Hello!" And even though he didn't reply, she knew he could hear her. Thank god, it was finally him.

Chapter 9

RECEPTION

Joshua's fierce and virile heart felt like it was stuck on overdrive, and he was having trouble breathing. He tried to relax his diaphragm, but it was useless.

Harmony smiled spastically. Her whole body was cooking from his heat, and she felt so small and insignificant she almost cried. He could never be interested in her. Oh god, please don't let him be married.

"When my wife gets here, tell her I'm in my office," sputtered Joshua to the receptionist, then he coughed to mask his suffocation. "I need to get some water."

"Oh, let me," the receptionist offered.

Gesturing no, Joshua turned to Harmony and in his most professional voice pronounced, "This is the Healing School. Are you here for the open house?"

Okay, so he was married. That actually relaxed her a tad. But why hadn't he introduced himself? "I'm a friend of Grace's," she offered, and she felt his mid-section flinch. My god, they were sleeping together! Well, good for Grace. "Grace told me anybody could come to this. And who are you?" she said, forcing what she hoped was a cordial smile.

Damn this woman, thought Joshua. He really didn't need this kind of trouble. "Joshua," answered Joshua, and he walked away.

The receptionist was astonished. "You're a little early. He probably has things to do," she said apologetically.

"No problem," said Harmony, biting the inside of her mouth to keep from laughing.

The main room of the school was the size of a ballroom with peach-colored walls, thick support columns running twenty feet up into beams the size of railroad ties, and no furniture. On the far end from the door, a couple of young women were setting up refreshment tables. "Hi, are you here for the party?" called one.

She sounded so friendly Harmony checked to see if there was someone standing behind her. "Who me?" she asked, seeing no one. "Yes, I'm a friend of Grace's."

The women looked concerned. "Grace called and said she couldn't make it. But please feel welcome. You're a little early."

"Thanks," said Harmony, wondering how to feel welcome. She was a stranger in a strange empty place where, at any moment, the man she had been waiting her whole life to meet might appear and hear her every thought. She wondered if Grace cancelled because she knew his wife would be here. Then she asked the refreshment women where the ladies' room was.

Harmony had learned that when anxiety hit, if she could sit alone in a bathroom stall things would get better. It wasn't quite as good as a closet, but an adult might be considered strange for asking if there were a closet she could hide in.

The bathroom was clean, with two stalls. She chose the one farthest from the door, and even though she didn't have to go, she pulled down her pants and sat. It was a toss-up which was more intolerable—the hot electricity of the missile or the terror rippling through her heart and up her throat. Breathe, Harmony, breathe. Think of something boring. The last article Joseph stole was a story about decorating with *tillandsias*, those marvelous rootless tropicals that live up in trees and get their food from the air. She had a collection of these charming epiphytes wired to the branches of her *ficus* tree at home, and she had written two sample pages: juicy descriptions of their flowers and misting instructions. Joseph had assigned the piece to that idiot Eleanor who'd killed every houseplant she'd ever owned and didn't know an epiphyte from a succulent. The fear was beginning to subside. Harmony wondered how long Grace had been having an affair with Joshua and if his wife knew. She remembered his hands from the bus and imagined holding one. She imagined how his skin would feel and how—

Bang, went the door as it slammed open. "Damn that Grace!" said a woman who sounded like the receptionist. Harmony held her breath while the woman and a companion dropped their stuff and turned on a faucet.

"Well, at least she called," said the companion who sounded like one of the refreshment women.

"That's not the point. She was supposed to be here to unlock. If I hadn't come early, that woman wouldn't have been able to get in."

"Jeez," said the refreshment woman, "who comes an hour early to a party?"

"And she's Grace's guest! I know we're supposed to be doing service, but I'm not Grace's handmaiden. If she invited someone, she should be here."

"Who is she anyway—the early bird?" said the refreshment woman.

"How should I know?" said the receptionist. "A better question is, *what* is she?"

Oh god, thought Harmony, they're thought-talkers and they heard me. Oh god.

"She's probably half-Black," said the refreshment woman.

"You think?" said the receptionist. "She made me uncomfortable."

"Why? Don't you have any Black friends?"

Harmony resumed breathing. Thank goodness, they were only bigots.

"I didn't mean that," said the receptionist, embarrassed. "She's just weird. Joshua must have thought so, too. I've never seen him be so rude."

"Hey!" yelled a third woman banging open the door. "Am I the only one who's here to work? I can use some help out here. People are starting to arrive."

Someone turned off the water; all three left; and Harmony pulled up her pants and flushed, even though the toilet was clean.

A crowd was gathered around the refreshment tables at the far end of the main room, and music, heavy on the bass and percussion, blasted over the sound system. "Are you going to join them?" asked a voice. Startled, Harmony looked around for the speaker. "Over here," said the voice. "We met at Luanne's."

"Crap," said Harmony, spotting the ghostly figure hovering about five feet above the entrance where she'd just come in. She decided to ignore it.

"Okay, if that's the way you want it," said the being, and it dissolved.

Harmony walked over to the refreshment tables and perused the spread while secretly scoping out the crowd. Almost no men. Then she felt the jolt—a dense energy surge from an entrance behind the sound system—and instantly she knew he was here. Female voices around the sound system went up in pitch the way they do at the sudden appearance of a potent man, and Harmony inhaled his smell—incense with a masculine bite. Yes, this guy had bite! She willed herself to breathe as her heart went into overdrive.

Joshua felt her instantly—the woman from the bus. It was like being hit by a seething hot whirlpool of energy, and her colors made him dizzy. I really don't need any trouble, he thought for the second time. His wife was due any minute, and if Grace showed, who knew what might happen. He walked around the perimeter of the room, greeting adoring students with a gentle touch to the shoulder, a paternal kiss to the top of a head, and he smiled as they melted. Joshua had missed lunch and had been looking forward to re-freshments, but he carefully avoided that part of the room. *She* was there. He could feel her eyes following him, examining his chest, his back, his buttocks. Oh no, she was on his crotch. He willed his blood to avoid the area, his body to relax, his lungs to breathe.

"Joshua?"

Judy! It was Judy. He grabbed her in an exaggerated hug and dipped and kissed her.

"Wow," she said once he'd pulled her up. "What did I do to deserve that?"

Several students observing the scene stared at the floor. They all wanted him—he knew this—and they could feed their fantasies just as long as Judy stayed away. Joshua enjoyed this—their crushes, Judy's surprise, their disap-pointment. It was like walking down the halls of Beale High School knowing he was adored and desired.

"Watch out."

Joshua looked around for the speaker.

"Over here."

He saw the ghostly being hovering in the air behind Judy, and he scowled.

"It's time, Joshua," said the being. "Go meet her." Then it dissolved.

The one thing Joshua hated more than any other was being told what to do. Revise that: being told to do something he didn't want to do. Sudden trips to the movies and saying yes to love were acceptable. But to say hello to a woman who could hear his every thought? Forget it. He wondered where Grace was and how he would finesse things between her and Judy.

"Oh, Joshua." It was Martha, who was in charge of reception. "I forgot to tell you—hi, Judy—Grace called and said she couldn't make it, but she finished all the paperwork you asked her to do in the office. It's nice to see you, Judy. You've lost all the weight from the baby."

Judy said thank you.

"Thank you, Martha," said Joshua, and Martha fought tears as she watched him stroke Judy's waist while guiding her to the refreshments.

"What would you like?" Joshua asked Judy. "I'm starved. I missed lunch."

"Let me get you something," said Judy, feeling warm from the dip and kiss. She liked it when he was possessive. "How about fruit and cheese?"

"Sounds great," said Joshua. "How's Emily?" he called as she moved away from him.

"She sends her da-da a wet kiss," called Judy, negotiating her way to the cheese table.

"Hello again," said a voice, and Joshua instinctively looked up.

"Down here," said Harmony. "I'm mortal."

"You certainly are," answered Joshua. What the hell? It was going to happen no matter what he did. "Are you having a good time? I hear Grace couldn't make it."

"My name is Harmony," said Harmony. "Harmony Rogers. I don't think I introduced myself. She was about to mention the bus, but Joshua's energetic wall slammed the front of her body.

As she'd grown older, Harmony had learned the etiquette to subtle communication—not to uninvitedly speak the unspoken. It was invasive. With Dr. Thompson, she had flaunted the rule because it was justified by the work and the fee. So, no, if he didn't want her to, she wouldn't mention the meeting on the bus.

"How's this?" said Judy offering Joshua a plate piled high with fruit, cheese, and bread. Then to Harmony, "Hello."

"Hello," said Harmony. "My name is Harmony Rogers. I was supposed to meet a friend here, but she didn't show."

Judy was relieved. She'd had a funny feeling watching her husband talking to this woman who looked like a short, Black Hillary Clinton, but probably it was paranoia. It was hard being married to the idol of many. It didn't matter how many times Joshua explained about transference and father/lover projections, she still felt threatened in this sea of female adoration for the man she loved.

"Grace told me about the school, and I was interested in finding out more," continued Harmony, and Judy kicked herself; the woman didn't even know Joshua. She really had to let this stuff go. "She said you do something with energy?" queried Harmony, sipping hot cider and raising her eyebrows.

"It's a three-year program. If you ask at reception, they can give you a brochure," said Joshua. And then, thank god, some first-year students on the other side of the room yelled "Joshua!" and he had to go say hello.

I'm fat, thought Harmony, watching Joshua caress Judy's pale shapely arm as they walked away. He appreciates a nice body. She would go on a diet and double her Kathy Smith sessions right after this party. Joshua had a nice walk. She gazed up and down his back, up and down—magnificent!

"You are driving me absolutely crazy," thought-talked Joshua, and Harmony grinned so hard she was afraid she might break her face.

Chapter 10

BALANCING THE BUDGET

Somewhere between the explosion with Joshua Gardner, reading the brochure, and looking at her yearly budget, Harmony decided that paying $4,000 annually for a weekend a month of workshops to learn how to touch people was insane—no matter how attractive the teacher. But clearly her life was missing something, so perhaps a career move was in order.

"I've got it all worked out," she told Dr. Thompson, pulling out her spreadsheet. "I'll work six more months at the magazine, cutting my expenses to the essentials—which is this column here; I'll get a part-time weekend job at a plant store, learn the business, and then, when the time is right, I'll open my own store. It'll probably be outside of New York City, so I'll have to quit therapy—which, lovely as it is, didn't make it into the essentials column anyway—which means this is my last session."

Dr. Thompson waited.

Harmony crossed and re-crossed her legs and studied a dirty spot on the couch. It was too bad Dr. Thompson's other patients didn't wash their hands before each session the way she did; people were no damned good.

"Is there anything else?" asked Dr. Thompson finally. She had gotten sensitive to Harmony's pauses, but this one was unprecedented.

"I'm having trouble going to work," answered Harmony softly. "And getting out of bed. I was going to double my Kathy Smith sessions, but I'm so late every morning I'm not even doing what I used to do. Probably I'll feel better once I start working at the plant store and fill in the part-time salary column on the sheet."

"Is that all?" asked Dr. Thompson. She would be nonjudgmental even if it killed her.

Harmony had heard that excessive exhaustion could be the result of inactivity. "I suppose I should exercise. I really like Kathy Smith. Her parents died when she was young, too. That's what started her on her fitness career; she began running like a maniac so her boyfriend wouldn't leave her. I've never liked running; my breasts are too big. But I do like Kathy Smith. I said that already, didn't I? Maybe if I got a heavy-duty bra."

"Do you feel depressed, Harmony?"

"I don't know. It's not like after Delilah died. It's just that I can't move."

"Are you still aroused?" This was the first session where Harmony wasn't attributing all her problems to the energetic missile between her legs.

"I don't know!" blurted Harmony, suddenly realizing she hadn't had a sexual thought since the night of the party. "The last time I felt really turned on was when I looked at Joshua Gardner, but then I saw the cost and I realized it's nuts. So, no, I'm not aroused. Do you think I'm cured of my presenting problem? That's what it's called, right? I've been browsing psychology books; the bookstore in my neighborhood has an excellent selection right next to the plant books. I'd consider that for a career change except for the fact that I hate people. No offense."

"None taken," said Dr. Thompson, swallowing hard to keep from laughing. "At the last session, you mentioned that Joshua could hear you think." Dr. Thompson had no idea why she was saying this, except that she'd learned to trust non sequitur impulses.

"Yes. I'm suddenly very tired."

"How do you know?"

"Because I want to go to sleep."

"No, how do you know he heard your thoughts?"

"Because he answered me. I mean I heard him think his answer to me. He said I was driving him crazy. God, I'm so tired I could go to sleep right here."

Harmony had explained that she felt other people's feelings as if they were her own, but somehow she knew when they belonged to the other person. Dr. Thompson felt lost. "Do you feel lost?" she asked Harmony.

"Yes! Yes!" erupted Harmony, popping on like a light bulb. "That's exactly how I feel. Maybe we should talk about where I'm going—my future direction? I could talk more about the plant store, and by the way, I hope you're okay with me quitting. Oh my god, I didn't even ask. I mean I know *you* must budget too, so this will probably decimate your spreadsheet. This is very narcissistic of me, isn't it? I read that in one of the books. I am *so* sorry."

Dr. Thompson was so tired, she had to fight to stay awake. This had to be empathic. How long had she been feeling other people's feelings, believing they were her own? No wonder she wanted to retire. "This exhaustion I'm feeling, I believe it might be—"

"Yes, yes, you do it too," interrupted Harmony. "Everybody feels each other's feelings. They just don't realize it. That's why I like plants so much. They know this. See, we're all the same entity; it's like other people and plants and everything are just parts of one body, so you can ask about anyone or anything as if you're asking 'what does my left big toe feel?' and somehow you know. You know what? I think I *do* want a few more sessions after all. God, I'm fickle. Sometimes I can get a little compulsive. I want to come back after today. Is that okay?"

Now Dr. Thompson felt like her head might explode. "Certainly you can come back. But we are almost out of time and I do want to suggest something."

"Oh god," said Harmony, wary after the experience with the Reiki idiot. "As long as I have the option to say no."

"Always," said Dr. Thompson. "That's a given. Here it is: I think you should go to this healing school. Just give it a try. See if you can pay by the weekend. Will you think about it?"

"Certainly," said Harmony, with no intention of giving it another thought. "Is the time up?"

"I'm afraid so," said Dr. Thompson. And before she could say, good-bye, see you in two weeks, Harmony was headed out the door.

Chapter 11

PLANT TALK

As a rule, Harmony limited her plant conversations to compliments and encouragement: "You are so beautiful. What a gorgeous flower. I just know, if you put your mind to it, you can discourage those mealybugs." And apologies: "Oh my goodness, how did you get so dirty? Forgive me, forgive me," as she washed the dust off the ficus. The plants responded with growth spurts and an abundance of blooms for the flowering plants. After concentrated appreciation—during feeding and pruning—they expanded, filling the living room with vibrant green waves of joyful light. Although Harmony felt that she was in conversation with her indoor garden, it occurred to her, after her session with Dr. T, that she never asked them any questions about themselves—another characteristic of narcissists, according to the last psychology book she'd browsed: It's *All About Me or Me, Me, Me!*, or some such title. She'd been too preoccupied with the characteristics list, trying to determine which ones were hers, to remember the correct title.

How to begin?

"Hello, plants," she announced from a cross-legged position in the middle of the living room floor. "I want to apologize for going so long without asking about you."

Silence.

Truthfully, she had never heard plants speak, but considering she had never asked for a response, that was understandable. She would be patient.

"So how are you?"

Silence.

"Okay, I see: the silent treatment. Well, I want you to know I do care what you feel and think, and I talked about you in therapy. I told Dr. T how you feel my feelings and I feel yours because we're one entity. Was I making that up or is it true?"

Silence.

"I really don't want to make things up. Especially with Dr. T. She is a very nice woman. You'd like her."

Silence.

"I understand that you might be angry that you've lived here all this time and I've never asked you a question. But I promise, if you'll answer now—anything you'd like me to know—I will listen as hard as I can to hear you. Is there something you'd like to say?"

Silence.

"I appreciate you all so much. I figured you'd know that by the way I praise you, but I'm sure you must want me to *know* you. I *want* to know you. So, please, talk to me."

Silence.

"Can I tell you a secret?"

Silence.

"I miss you. I know that sounds crazy because you're right here, and I'm right here, but I do. I miss hearing you, knowing what you think, knowing if you need anything that I'm not giving you. Did you know Delilah died? I never even told you. That's why she's gone. Do you understand about death? What a silly question—you see it all the time. Well, I say I know about death, but the truth is I don't. I don't understand a damned thing. For instance, why everybody I love is dead and I'm not. Why I'm even here. What's the point? I know I could get a cat—and then the point would be to take care of the cat—but I don't want another pet. I want— I want—. I would really like you to talk to me."

Chapter 12

CATS ON A POLE

The first class at the healing school was a Saturday afternoon in August—the week after Al Gore and George W. Bush had been nominated for president. Grace said graduates and third-year students sat in on first-year classes as assistant teachers, but if Harmony was uncomfortable with that because of their work connection, Grace wouldn't come. Grace had just volunteered to work for Gore, so she was secretly glad when Harmony said she would prefer she stay away. Harmony was secretly glad Grace was glad; Grace could do whatever she liked with Joshua on her own time. But after much contemplation and wondering what Kathy Smith would do, she'd decided to invest in one weekend—one weekend of class time with another thought-talker—with no interference from a work colleague who was having an affair with the object of her investment.

"So what's cooking?" asked Joshua, surveying the circle of new students. When he got to Harmony, he moved quickly on. Harmony watched how he lingered on the frightened or needy students, and she was flattered. Also, this meant she could linger on Joshua as much as she pleased. She drank in his pectorals visible under his old T-shirt. And she knew he knew just how well they showed because he examined himself—just as she was doing now—every morning before he left the house. She knew he was nervous and was avoiding looking at her, and this flattered her also.

A long-waisted, long-necked string bean of a girl with long bangs was talking about her abandonment issues and how, because of that, she was afraid to become part of a group where people could leave her. It sounded like she was trying to get some kind of assurance that everybody would like her no matter how annoying she was.

"Why don't you and I blow this joint and go somewhere and make out?" Harmony thought-talked to Joshua, just for fun, and Joshua had a coughing fit. Thank goodness Dr. T had pushed this. This was *really* going to be fun.

Another woman with a torso shaped like a giant potato said she had been sexually abused when she was four and she could no longer live with the secret. She said she had come to the school to learn to love her body and help the world.

Joshua didn't say or think much. Harmony watched him just listen to people and ignore the fact that she'd just thought-talked about her own need to have him naked on top of her, and then she wondered if she'd gone too far. It was just that it was so exciting to sit opposite the first person she'd ever met who spoke her secret language. But she vowed to be good and try to listen to all the people.

The next person was a very pretty, sweet-faced girl in her early twenties. She had long, blonde hair and a dancer's body. She said she'd had cancer—a tumor in her stomach—and Joshua had helped heal her in private sessions. Now she wanted to learn to be a healer and help others.

Harmony popped to attention. Cora. Somehow she had to get Cora to go to Joshua, and she had no idea what to do. She could ask Grace to help, but what if—

"And what about you, Harmony?" said Joshua suddenly, and Harmony grabbed her heart.

"Excuse me? I'm sorry, I wasn't listening. What?"

"Why are *you* here?" asked Joshua, looking deep into her eyes for the first time.

"I have no idea," answered Harmony, and the whole class laughed.

"You don't know," said Joshua.

"That's right," answered Harmony, feeling a cylinder of energy from his mid-section shoot into her own where it spread like the roots of a tree. Harmony shuddered, but she couldn't move.

"Gotcha!" thought-talked Joshua, his eyes sparkling. Then he turned to the rest of the class. "Who here believes they are not in a cage?"

The students looked blank.

"My body feels like a cage," said the overweight potato woman timidly.

"That's only part of it," snapped Joshua, and the woman blushed. "By the time you all graduate, you will look back and see where you are now for what it is. But don't worry about it right now."

The class shifted uncomfortably.

Joshua said that after the lunch break, they would practice "table work," a form of laying-on of hands for healing purposes. He said that during lunch, everyone should contemplate whether their soul needed to be the healer or the healee in this exercise, but not to worry because eventually everybody would play both roles.

As the class gathered in front of the elevator to go to lunch, Harmony held back. A morning of group activity was sufficient. And she would not be bound by the "rats in a cage" mentality that you had to eat with the group. She was an independent thinker.

"That's *your* cage," thought-talked Joshua as he stepped into the elevator.

Harmony pretended not to hear, and she pulled out her brown bag lunch and ate, sitting on the floor. When she was finished, she lay down on one of the mats scattered around the room and closed her eyes. In no time, she was in a backyard with an old-fashioned well. There was a mean-eyed old woman sitting in a lawn chair drinking tea and, next to her, Joshua's wife was nursing Delilah. Suddenly, the sky darkened and the old woman screamed, "Save the baby! Save the baby!" In response, Joshua's wife threw Delilah down the well. "No!" screamed Harmony, diving in after her. Then suddenly, she was at the bottom of the well with her arms spread to catch. And *thwunk*! Delilah, who mid-fall had turned into a baby, landed in her arms. "She's mine," said a voice, and Harmony looked up to see Joshua falling from the sky, arms outstretched to take Delilah. And as Harmony handed her over, she woke up.

***

Joshua lowered the lights as third-year assistants set up massage tables all over the room. "You've had plenty of time to think about it," he said. "Will everyone who feels they should act as the healer in this exercise, please raise their hands."

Harmony was groggy from her nap and suddenly realized she hadn't given one thought to the matter. But she raised her hand because she felt gassy from her brown bag lunch, and she was afraid if she got too relaxed, she'd fart.

"All right, healees, choose your healers."

As people pushed and shoved to find a partner, Harmony flashed back to fifth-grade ballroom dancing class. "Boys, choose your partners," command-ed Mr. Charles, and for thirty seconds there was pandemonium as the boys rushed the girls, grabbing anyone who was pretty or non-threatening or not-fat and light-skinned. And at the end, it was always the same two girls left behind: the girl from the last row in the third grade who was now obese, and Harmony, who hated to run and therefore was very bad at sports, but loved to dance. "One last dance with Daddy," her father used to say before the accident. Harmony stared straight ahead with a frozen smile, wishing she were dead.

"Will you be my healer?" asked the blonde girl who'd had stomach cancer, and Harmony catapulted back to the present.

"What?" she answered. "I mean, thank you, I'd be happy to—. I mean yes. Of course. Where do you want to do it?"

The girl looked at her quizzically, then pointed to the table right beside them.

"Great," said Harmony. "We don't have to travel."

Joshua told the healees to lie face-up on their tables with their eyes closed. He said one of the assistants would be leading the exercise. Then he stepped into the shadows to watch.

"Will all the healers please stand at your healee's feet," said the assistant, a stocky woman with the voice of a speech teacher. And as the healers moved into place, the room shifted into order. "Now look at this divine being lying in front of you," continued the assistant. "Really look. Fall in love."

Harmony stared as hard as she could. The blonde girl was very pretty, but Harmony sure didn't feel in love. Mostly she just craved fresh air. They hadn't done anything, and already the room stank—fear, anger, jealousy, re-sentment—all that toxic stuff everybody felt but pretended they didn't. In fact, the more people pretended, the worse feelings stank, and this room smelled like a dump. Harmony tried to mouth-breathe and, following the assistant's instructions, placed the palms of her hands on the soles of the blonde girl's feet. There was a surge of energy, and Harmony closed her eyes, feeling like she'd just submerged her hands in warm, streaming water. She had never touched anyone but her father's feet, and that was after the ac-cident, and they felt like dead fish. She was just starting to enjoy herself when the assistant directed them to move their hands to the tops of the per-son's ankles. There was a nervous vibration there—like an egg just before something hatched. Harmony knew this from her visit to the petting zoo the morning of the accident. Her father had put an egg in her hands and had told her to hold it very gently because it held a baby. And as she was holding it, she felt a surge of heat come out of her palms and the egg cracked and a baby chick pushed out. That was the last time she remembered seeing her mother smile.

"When you're ready, as slowly as you can, move your hands to your person's knees," directed the assistant. And a few minutes later, to the pelvic bones, the ribs, the collar bone, and down the arms. Harmony found the whole thing so interesting, she almost forgot the stink. But that ended when they were doing chakras. The assistant said to put one hand just above the pubic bone and the other on the mid-section, and a geyser of stink shot up from the blonde girl's stomach, hitting Harmony square in the face. She gagged and turned her head, afraid she was going to throw up. It smelled like the sourness Joseph gave off every time he was about to steal an idea, plus wet dog, dead foot skin, dirty socks, and rotten hard-boiled eggs. The last three smells she associated with fear. The whole thing smelled like Cora before her chemotherapy, and in one horrible flash, Harmony knew the cancer was still there. Should she tell the girl? But what if she was mistaken? How come Joshua hadn't picked this up? What the hell was wrong with the girl's doctors, telling her she was cured?! Harmony felt like she was going to explode.

From the shadows, Joshua looked for the source of the fireball light. Of course—he should have guessed. He stared at Harmony, glowing red with yellow and orange flames leaping out of her heart, lighting up all the tables around her. It looked like anger, but it was breathtaking. Joshua was mesmerized. What the hell was going on?

"I told you, it's time," said the ghostly being above Joshua's head. He shot it a dirty look, and it disappeared into the ether.

The exercise finally ended, the lights came up, and Harmony suddenly realized the stink she was smelling was her own. She was drenched with sweat and felt like crying.

"Thank you," said the blonde girl opening her eyes as if emerging from the sweetest sleep. "That was wonderful. Have you done this before?"

Harmony felt stupid. "No," she answered. "By the way, I'm Harmony.

What's your name?"

"Roxana," said the blonde girl. "That was one of the nicest experiences I've ever had. Would it be all right if I hugged you?"

Harmony wasn't that comfortable with strangers. "Sure," she said, closing her eyes and opening her arms. And ever so carefully, Roxana wrapped her arms around her and pulled her into her heart. Harmony flashed to the cat on the telephone pole outside her house—the way he looked when the big fireman first made contact, cuddling him in his arms as he gently carried him down the ladder and lowered him to the ground. The cat tried to pretend it didn't matter, but Harmony saw that nanosecond of relief before he twitched his tail, turned his back, and ran away from everyone.

"Cats on a pole," said the ghostly being, watching Joshua watching Harmony. "It's time."

Chapter 13

ENERGY SEX

"I can't go back there," said Harmony.

"Why not?" asked Dr. Thompson. "You said he could thought-talk. Isn't that what you've wanted?"

"Yes, but he told Roxana she's cured, and I smelled the cancer, and it's $4,000. And the only man in the class is gay. Why is it wherever I go the men are gay?"

"Joshua isn't gay."

Harmony blushed. "No, he certainly isn't. But everyone's pretending all the time. Nobody tells the truth." Harmony felt like her head was going to explode.

"Isn't that just what people do?"

"What?"

"Well, imagine how it would be if everybody always said exactly what they feel—believing it's true, when in fact it's not always the truth."

"What do you mean?" Harmony felt dazed and scared as she suddenly remembered the dream where Joshua had taken Delilah.

"Well, for instance, sometimes you feel that you hate Cora, right?"

Harmony nodded, swallowing fear and willing the dream to go away.

"But when you thought Roxana had found a miracle cure for her cancer, your first thought was to save Cora. Does that sound like hate?"

Harmony wished she could hear a little better. How dare Joshua take her baby?!

"And you think Joseph disrespects you because he steals your ideas and gives them to other people, but if your ideas are good enough to steal, I would guess he actually respects you. Also, if you were working on stories, do you think you'd have the energy to go to this school? You said they meet a weekend a month, and it's taken you almost three weeks to recover from your first class. By the way, are you sleeping any better with that medication?" Dr. Thompson made a mental note to check this Joshua Gardner's credentials—find out if he had any accredited psychology training—before she went on sabbatical. She was nervous about leaving her patients for such an extended period, but she needed to refuel and a sabbatical was a good compromise to retiring.

"I only took one pill," said Harmony, blinking hard and suddenly forgetting her dream. "I'm better now." She took a deep breath and wondered why she'd been so frightened. "So what you're saying is that Joseph is doing me a favor by stealing my ideas. He just doesn't know it."

Dr. Thompson smiled. "People don't always know the whole picture or what they really feel—that's what keeps me in business."

Harmony laughed.

Dr. Thompson was glad she hadn't retired. You just never know who you're going to love. She knew Harmony heard this last thought because she blushed and looked away. "Well, our time is almost up. Is there anything we've missed? You know I'll be away until the first of January."

"Oh god, we could all be dead by then," said Harmony, rolling her eyes.

"I don't generally take such long breaks—"

"I was just joking," interrupted Harmony, feeling guilty for upsetting Dr. T at the last minute before her vacation. "I can't think that far ahead is all. New president, new world. You never know what'll be."

"That's certainly true," said Dr. Thompson, wondering if there was something she wasn't picking up on. "Well, if you have an emergency—"

"I don't have emergencies," said Harmony. "And I can use the dough I'll save on your salary." She launched an energetic hug. "Don't worry. I was just joking," she thought-talked.

"I know," thought-talked Dr. Thompson touching her heart.

"I'll see you next year," said Harmony.

***

Harmony felt a little guilty for keeping her energy meetings with Joshua a secret from Dr. Thompson, but she wasn't sure they were real. In Dr. T's absence, she enjoyed experimenting and not having to avoid talking about it in therapy. The meetings had begun with thoughts during the day. In the middle of slush pile rejections, she'd suddenly think about kissing Joshua, and before she knew it, her lips swelled, hot with energy, and she had the distinct feeling he was energetically kissing her back. In the months that followed, she was especially careful to avoid such thoughts around Grace, who dropped by occasionally to say hello. Grace seemed to feel a special, almost possessive, connection to Harmony now that Harmony was enrolled in her school. Harmony listened for Grace's thoughts about Joshua, but the woman hardly thought at all. She'd make an excellent therapist.

Cora finished her chemotherapy, but the tumor was still there. Harmony casually suggested she try some alternative treatments, but Cora wouldn't hear of it. Her main concern was when her hair would grow back so she could get rid of the damned wig.

Joseph fell in love with a young man in accounting, and in a fit of good feeling promised Harmony she could write a sidebar to the rescued houseplants piece. But at the last minute, he changed his mind and gave it to the new intern who was his new boyfriend's niece.

The first time Harmony and Joshua made love—if you can call it that—was a week after her second month of classes. Harmony enjoyed thinking about Joshua's body. She'd envision his back or his buttocks. Sometimes his chest, his throat, his mouth. She'd close her eyes and call whatever part she fancied into view. She would do this in the evening, lying on her couch listening to music. She especially liked doing it while listening of the score to *South Pacific*—most particularly the ballad, "Younger Than Springtime Are You." She knew she wasn't so young anymore; she was approaching her forty-third birthday. But that made the fantasy of Joshua thinking those lyrics and desiring her even sexier. Sometimes, she imagined he was hearing her doing this.

One evening, after a hard day of mindless tidying, she was feeling tired and in the mood to cause trouble. And since her parents were dead and she had no close friends to annoy, not to mention that she was on hiatus from Kathy Smith, she decided to try an experiment: She turned on *South Pacific*, lay down on the couch, closed her eyes, and concentrated on Joshua's crotch.

In short order she felt a well of seething hotness in her uterus—the second chakra. It was almost as if she were about to get menstrual cramps, only far more pleasurable. In her mind's eye, she saw Joshua. He was at some kind of dinner party with a bunch of people. His face turned beet red; then all pictures disappeared and there was only red energy—his and hers. "Please," she begged him. "I want you inside me." Her whole body felt like a uterus—hot, open, alive with desire.

"Do you really want this?" Joshua asked her.

"Please," she begged. And then it came. Not exactly a penis, but energy in the shape of one, dipping slowly, so gently into the seething pool of heat in her uterus. "Oh my god!" gasped Harmony. And he dipped and pulled out, and dipped again. Harmony wondered if she could get pregnant this way, and she felt Joshua laugh, which jiggled her uterus. "Oh my god," she sighed when it was over. And in her mind's eye, she was lying with him, his arms around her, his head on her heart. "I think Roxana may still have cancer," she said, apropos of nothing. And she felt him disappear.

***

It was mid-October when first year met for the third time. As before, Joshua looked around the circle and asked, "What's cooking?" They were getting more comfortable with each other so secret rivalries and resentments began to surface. The sexually abused potato woman sniped at the younger thin women and accused Joshua of favoring them. Then the only man in the class revealed that he was gay, like this was a secret, and when a couple of women laughed, he was so offended, he threatened to quit the school. Joshua reprimanded the women and said that everybody's process deserves respect. Then the women got upset at the gay guy for his habit of reveling in people's discomfort when some embarrassing truth was suddenly exposed. He answered, "Then that should make you all more sensitive to what a big risk it was for me to reveal my homosexuality—even if everybody already knew." He said it "gave people ammunition" against him. Joshua asked if he considered life a battlefield, and he shut up. Joshua smiled kindly and said the guy was where he was, and we all need space to grow.

Harmony found this conversation boring and kept feeling for any sign of their energetic affair, but Joshua looked at her blankly.

Somebody asked where Roxana was, and Joshua stared at his lap. "I'm afraid she had a recurrence and had to have emergency surgery. She's recovering nicely, as far as I know, and if any of you want to send a card, Martha can give you the address at the break."

Harmony had a funny feeling. Thank goodness they'd found the cancer, but she wondered what alerted them. *Who* had alerted them? Had Joshua heard her worry? No matter. Thank goodness they'd found it.

As was becoming her custom, at lunch break, Harmony stayed behind and ate from a brown bag on the floor of the classroom. Only this time, a couple of others stayed too. "This is a lot cheaper than the restaurants," said one of them. Harmony nodded, and as soon as she'd finished, lay face down on the mat so nobody would talk to her.

***

"Nobody move," said Joshua. People were slouched against walls, lying on mats all over the room, in a post-lunch stupor. "Does everyone know what a puppy pile is?" he asked with mischievous glint in his eyes, and some people groaned and others moaned, "What is it?"

"Assistants, against the wall. You don't get to do this," said Joshua, herding people. "Everyone else, to the center of the floor. No, no, don't get up. Stay just as you are. Slide. Now pile. That's it—pile on top of each other like puppies."

There were arms and legs landing on bones and soft places it was best not to identify. People flopped and laughed, heads on stomachs, breasts on butts, elbows in mouths.

"Okay," said Joshua, "now just lie there. Enjoy the contact."

The pile heaved a communal sigh of pleasure. Harmony wondered whose crotch her head was in, but it seemed rude to check, so she looked straight ahead, watching Joshua.

"Your dress," whispered the potato woman on her right, pulling Harmony's dress down to cover her legs.

"Whoops," said Harmony, eyes glued on Joshua. "I forgot there's a boy in the room."

Joshua locked on her eyes and thought-talked, "After what you did."

"What?!" thought-talked Harmony, but Joshua didn't answer. He just stared. "Oh my god, you mean it was real?" thought-gasped Harmony.

"How could you?" thought-talked Joshua. And Harmony slapped her hands over her mouth, choking on laughter. Then suddenly she remembered the others. "They can't hear this," thought-talked Joshua, incredulous.

"Are you sure?"

"Yeah."

Harmony strained to see faces; everybody was oblivious, eyes closed, drugged. Joshua shook his head and just stared at her.

At first, this felt nice, and Harmony returned his gaze. But suddenly it didn't feel nice. A surge came out of Joshua's eyes, penetrating her own and locking. Harmony's smile froze, then shattered. Her heart froze, her limbs contorted, and she curled in, seeking refuge from his stare.

"That's what real contact feels like," thought-talked Joshua. "Are you ready for it?"

"It's better to wear pants," murmured the potato woman without opening her eyes.

"Yeah," answered Harmony, shaking off Joshua and looking at her. "We wouldn't want the boys to see our petticoats."

"Didn't think so," thought-talked Joshua, and turned away.

Chapter 14

CONTACT PHOBIA

Weird, thought Harmony as she trudged up her stairs. It had been a long day and probably the reason she couldn't remember the last hour or so of it—everything after Joshua had confirmed that their energy affair was real—was exhaustion. But she also felt powerful. Validated by Joshua's thought-talking. What a fantastic way to have sex! She would have to experiment more.

Click-click, a lock cylinder turning, door opening, assaultive lights blasting into the dark hallway. "Harmony?" It was her neighbor on the third floor. The woman had dog hearing.

"Hi, Bella," said Harmony, hoping whatever it was wouldn't take too long.

Bella hugged her pink terrycloth robe closed and pointed to the towel around her wet hair. "Never call me vain."

"I wouldn't think of it, Bella," said Harmony, waiting, yearning for the privacy of her apartment. "What's up?"

"You haven't told me if you're coming to Thanksgiving," said Bella. "The orphans' dinner."

God, how she hated that name. "Oh, gee, Bella, thanks so much, but I'm afraid I have other plans." Harmony had gone to this orphans' Thanksgiving for the last two years, and she couldn't imagine putting herself through that for a third time and exerting the requisite social energy to be with a roomful of strangers. "I'm sorry I didn't RSVP. I've been really busy at work."

Bella looked at her deeply. Harmony twisted, as if to continue up the stairs. "Sweetheart," said Bella. Harmony felt a golf-ball-size knot in her throat. "No pressure. I just thought if you were alone—"

"That is so thoughtful of you, Bella. Really. But you shouldn't worry about me. I'm fine."

"Since your mom died, and the dog—"

"Really, Bella, I've got plans."

"Well, give us a hug then," said Bella, spreading her fat maternal arms, even though the gesture exposed her nightgown and a good deal of private skin.

Harmony liked Bella. She really did. But her insistence on hugs was a constant irritant. Trying to suppress a full-body cringe, Harmony leaned in at the shoulders.

"There now," said Bella, seemingly oblivious to the adrenaline coursing through Harmony's stomach. "If you change your mind, just stop by. There's always room for one more."

"Thanks, Bella," said Harmony, trying to politely disconnect her body from Bella's. "I certainly will."

When she got to the fourth floor, Harmony unlocked her door as quietly as she was able. She stepped inside, closed the door after her, bolted it, and sank to the floor.

Chapter 15

EMPTY

The most difficult time, although he would never admit it, was after everyone had left. Joshua transformed into a sorrowful wanderer in the immense empty classroom, picking up used paper cups, a glove left behind. He'd promised Judy to be home by 7:30 to sing "Happy Birthday" to Emily. It was ridiculous. What does a baby know of birthdays? But Judy was on one of her missions to enforce her picture of a perfect family. Joshua stared at the floor where the puppy pile had been and spied a couple of coins and a set of keys—somebody was going to have a hard night. He pocketed the coins and tossed the keys in the lost and found box with the glove. Then he just stared. Maybe he'd call Frederic and invite him to meet for a drink. Grace had said she was busy this weekend or he'd give her a spur-of-the-moment visit. These weekends were wonderful, but when they were over, there was always a vacuum, an invisible, immemorial fog of death—kind of like when he was making love to new girls every weekend. But he was better than that now. He was a teacher, a helper, a husband. These feelings were merely part of a puerile past—nothing to dwell on; the less attention he gave them, the faster they'd dissipate. He checked his watch; if he left right now, he'd be home an hour early, and Judy would be pleased. He noticed a footprint on the cushion of one of his new red chairs. Frowning, he reached to brush it off, and then stopped himself. No, that was the old Joshua—the pre-baby, pre-marriage man who had to have everything just so. The thing he hated most about Judy was her sloppiness. He looked at the footprint, then walked away.

He turned off the lights and decided to check his messages before locking up. He'd still be home forty-five minutes early.

His office was neat and simple, just the way he liked it. Massage table on the far side, a black leather roll-out couch for when he stayed over, a small glass table with black wrought iron legs which he used as a desk and a matching chair. Shelves full of gifts from his students and Judy: several stuffed animals, monogrammed coffee mugs, colorful ceramics, a small Tibetan singing bowl, and a wooden Buddha . . . It had been a long time since he'd spoken to Rinpoche. How had they fallen out of touch? He always enjoyed their conversations. He would have to give him a call one of these days—maybe when work lightened up, maybe on the break between school terms, maybe after the holidays.

The answering machine was blinking. There were six calls asking for school brochures, and he transferred them to Grace's mailbox. Then one in a voice so raspy he had to listen twice to realize who it was: Roxana! He called her back immediately.

Roxana said she was okay. Her throat was just sore from the intubation. Joshua asked what medicines she was being given, what follow-up; then he listened intently. The surgeon hadn't found anything he could get, so they'd started her on an aggressive, three-drug chemotherapy. "Did they give you time to meditate?" he asked, and Roxana recounted the cold room with fluorescent lights, the metal chair, and by the time she got to the draft from the window that never closed properly, Joshua was incensed. "I'll be there as soon as I can. I'm leaving now." Roxana protested that this really wasn't necessary, but Joshua wouldn't hear of it. He would rebalance her endocrine system, jump-start her thymus, restore her light. These doctors! They were mechanics. Somewhere between taking the Hippocratic Oath and becoming a cog in the money-driven, overworked, under-staffed medical machine, they'd forgotten the "art" of healing and the well-being of the patient. But it wasn't too late. Joshua turned off the lights in his office, and locked the elevator on his way down. And it wasn't until he was walking up the stairs at the 168th Street subway stop that he remembered he'd forgotten to call Judy.

"It was an emergency," he tried to explain later that evening. "Judy, I just couldn't say no. I know how difficult this is for you, but this is my work. I can't say no when people need me. I wish I could, but I can't do it."

"What about when *I* need you?" barked Judy, stomping the pedal on the garbage can so the top slammed into the wall. She dumped the stale cake that had been sitting out for Joshua for the past four hours. "What about when your daughter needs you?"

Joshua sank into the kitchen chair and held his face in his hands. She was never going to understand. This commitment wasn't his choice; it was his destiny. Somehow he would have to learn to tolerate being misunderstood because of Judy's limitations. Although he was no longer in love with her, he did value her. He was a good man pulled in too many directions.

After Judy went to bed, Joshua crept into Emily's room to kiss her good-night. When she looked up and smiled, he saw his own twinkly eyes, and his heart burst. "Hi, baby; happy birthday," he whispered, picking her up and hugging her. "Daddy's sorry he didn't get home in time for your cake. But I know you understand."

"Da-da," cooed Emily, resting her head in the crook of his neck.

"Oh, my beautiful baby," murmured Joshua, smelling the top of her sweet baby head. "Oh, my beautiful baby." And for a few minutes he didn't feel so alone.

Chapter 16

THANKSGIVING

Harmony had never cared much about politics, but she did like Hillary Rodham Clinton, and the fact that Hillary had won the New York Senate seat was a small consolation for what some considered to be the stealing of the presidential election by the Republicans. Harmony liked Hillary's quiet strength. She had even bought her book, *It Takes a Village*, and intended to read it someday. She thought Hillary got a raw deal with Bill and she wondered if Joshua's wife was anything like her. She wondered if having energy sex with somebody else's husband was as bad as what Monica Lewinsky had done.

Harmony was lonely, and holidays were particularly difficult. Bella had invited her to that "orphan party" . . . They even used to make a special dinner for Delilah. "Yes, I'd like to come. Is it too late?" she practiced out loud. But inside she felt a full-body cringe as bad as when Bella insisted on hugging her. She couldn't do it. Not the hugs, the air kisses with complete strangers, the standing too close, and particularly not the inevitable dinner talk: political diatribes about George W. Bush and how the world as we know it had come to an end.

What to do? She'd already rented three movies from an out-of-the-way video store. Maybe they would take her mind off things—like the fact that most of the population was beguiled by the mass slaughter of large birds who had done nothing but graze and gobble.

"Because of their widely spaced eyes," said the Internet article, "they have poor binocular vision and depth perception; they see very little in front of them with both eyes at the same time, which makes it difficult for them to determine the relative size and distance of objects. However, movement makes them alert." Harmony could relate.

She fixed herself a bowl of raw oatmeal with soy milk, peeled a banana, and as she ate it, read the jackets of the two video comedies; the actors were people she'd never heard of. The third movie was a spur-of-the moment pick—what the hey, she would never go to that video store again, except to return them—an erotic movie made "by and for women."

"Let's see what these are," she said to the plants. Then she loaded the first movie, the second, then the third into the VCR—fast-forwarding for about thirty seconds each. The comedies were car chases and slapstick. The erotic movie was a series of well-built young men who looked more interested in their own pecs than the women they were ostensibly seducing by undulating and taking off their clothes. "Damn," said Harmony, hitting the off button. She finished her oatmeal and looked in the refrigerator for something else that required no effort.

When she'd started her job, Harmony had been a big fan of *Your Garden.* Her mother was still alive then. Sometimes Mrs. Rogers worried about Harmony being alone after she died, so she was relieved when Harmony found something that made her happy. Harmony loved plants, and for years had read the magazine cover-to-cover, savoring the lush gardens, dense with color and every hue of green imaginable. Even though she never articulated the fantasy to herself, she realized from her disappointment during the first year that she'd hoped *Your Garden* would be a surrogate family. She had imagined it would be a place bursting with life and color; garden writers with rosy cheeks who would invite everyone out to their country homes to sip tea and swap gardening stories. She thought she might find people who would welcome her ideas, and she would be a valued member of a team. Even though she still pitched an occasional idea, she knew she was doing it with secret spite—just to prove how awful Joseph was and to scoff at him for rejecting her offer to do twice as much work. The fact is she no longer even liked the magazine and didn't really need to read it—or even show up more than a few hours a day—to do her job. She had more free time than she'd ever had in her life and was being paid a full-time salary. Why did this feel like purgatory?

She reconsidered calling Bella and saying she wanted to come to Thanksgiving after all. Or what if she went to a bar? Bad idea. No contact with strangers in a shared space where everybody else wanted contact was even worse than physical contact with strangers. She could only imagine who went to a bar on Thanksgiving and she despised alcohol. Also, the last time she'd tried to have casual sex had been one of the loneliest experiences of her life. The sex itself was fine; the man had been a generous and gentle lover. It was what happened during her orgasm. Harmony loved orgasms—the explosion, releasing tidal waves of energy pulsing into new explosions throughout her body—it was the one time she felt whole. But just at the moment when she felt out of her mind, roaring with pleasure, pulsing and vibrating, an open chasm ready to merge with him, the man turned white and limp. "What's the matter?" pleaded Harmony, willing herself compassionate. "Whatever it is, it's all right," she promised, almost believing this herself. But he wouldn't talk. All he said was, "This is too much. Sorry." And he put on his clothes and left. If this had been the first time she'd seen that reaction, she might have chalked it up to the man's peculiarity. But it had happened every time she'd had sex—even if they'd gone on several dates and she'd warned him ahead of time that she felt things big. First, he would be excited at her passion, then horrified as she surrendered to it. It seemed sex was the fastest way to get rid of a man, and finally she'd sworn to be with somebody who spoke her secret language or be celibate.

Although she was physically aroused all the time from the missile between her legs, she was only out-of-her-mind desirous of contact for one week of every month—just before ovulation—this week. But it wasn't worth picking up a stranger. She contemplated buying a new houseplant, but all the markets were closed and her usually bustling Lower Eastside neighborhood felt like a morgue.

She was lying on her couch wondering if she should get a cat when she felt the energy. She knew it was Joshua from the smell: incense laced with a masculine bite. But this time, it was different. She hadn't invited it; it had insinuated *her* into *it*—into Joshua's fantasy: As if in an awake dream, she was suddenly sitting bare-breasted in the middle of class. Harmony had always thought herself disproportionately large for her size, so she knew this wasn't *her* fantasy. As she sat there, one by one her classmates crawled into her lap and nursed.

"Gross!" she said out loud. Then feeling an unseen Joshua recoil with embarrassment, "I'm sorry; I'm sorry. It's fine. It just surprised me." And the nursing continued. She could feel his excitement, and that was nice. But try as she might, she could not see him. Since this was *his* fantasy, there was logic to that. Finally, everyone finished nursing and left the room. Harmony felt Joshua move his attention from her breasts to her lips which swelled with blood in response. She wanted him to kiss her, but it seemed he just wanted to look. Okay, she thought. He's entitled to his fantasy. And fantasies weren't real infidelity, right?

Harmony had stopped initiating energy sex after Joshua's reprimand during the last class, but now that *he'd* initiated, maybe it was okay. So late that night, as she lay in bed feeling the longing, she surrendered. She closed her eyes and let her uterus flood with molten energy, then her heart and her arms and hands. Her neck arched and she hungered for the touch of his lips.

"No," said Joshua.

"What?" she said aloud, opening her eyes.

And in a voice as clear as if he were in the room, he said, "If you want me, *you* come to *me*."

Harmony pondered this. Yes, he had a point: In all of her fantasies, she was demanding that *he* come to *her*. It had never occurred to her that she could do the traveling.

She closed her eyes and, in no time, was in one of the loveliest bedrooms she'd ever seen. The curtains were white lace, waving gently in a breeze, and the comforter on the bed was warm blues, greens, and purples in a patchwork pattern. As she lowered herself on top of Joshua, her buttocks burned. If he didn't touch her there, she was going to go insane. "Please," she begged.

Joshua opened his eyes, awakened out of a deep sleep, saw Harmony's subtle body, felt the pressure of her on top of him. "I beg you," pleaded Harmony, and ever so gently, Joshua put one hand, then the other, on her buttocks. The heat was intense, but it didn't hurt. Harmony roared, pulsing, vibrating, quivering with joy and pleasure, an open chasm inviting him to enter, and Joshua wasn't afraid.

After it was over and Harmony had disappeared, Joshua turned to look at Judy. Still asleep. Thank god. He wiped his brow and wondered what the hell he was doing.

On the Lower Eastside, Harmony sank into the first peaceful sleep she'd had since Delilah died.

Chapter 17

TRIBE

The next month went by in a blink. Harmony did her managing work with such good-humored efficiency that Joseph wondered if she was in love. But he knew it was none of his business.

Cora began to like Harmony and made a special effort to compliment her rescued houseplants.

Grace smiled. She knew how magical the school was, and she gave Harmony space to have her experience.

"So what's cooking?" asked Joshua perusing the circle with twinkly flirtatious eyes, lingering on Harmony who smiled and twinkled right back. Double takes and raised eyebrows shot around the room, but Joshua and Harmony were unbothered. "We're going to have a slight change this weekend," continued Joshua, enjoying the curiosity. "The second half of this morning's session and the whole afternoon will be led by the assistants. I'll be in the other classroom working with second year."

A discontented rumble erupted around the circle, and the gay guy yelled, "Just a minute here. I'm not paying $4,000 tuition to be taught by student teachers!"

"Calm down, everyone; calm down," said Joshua. He'd been expecting this and was prepared. "We go through this every year. You build an attachment, and then I bust it. That's how it works. It's got to be busted; otherwise you'll start believing the work is about me instead of staying with yourselves. You think it's got to be a certain way—that's your cage. This happens with every class."

There was a lot of grumbling, but Joshua sounded sincere. Maybe he was more altruistic than some of them had imagined. A few had begun to believe he was on a power trip—that he got off on the adoration. But here he was openly addressing it. Maybe he had a point and they should trust his decision.

"But what if there's a problem that the assistants don't know how to handle?" said the string-bean girl with abandonment issues.

"Like what?" Joshua smiled. He knew she had a crush on him. The girl blushed and didn't answer. "Besides, as a few of you may know by now, I know what's going on everywhere. If there's a problem, I'll know and I'll come bail you out. I'm omniscient!" He grinned, and everyone laughed. "So, as I was saying, what's cooking?"

Several people talked about the inner changes they were experiencing and how threatening it was for their boyfriends or husbands. Joshua said they would just have to weather it—to remember that if one partner is willing to know herself, then even if the other partner is resistant, he will grow too. So the fact that they were making their partners uncomfortable was a service.

A woman who spoke in perpetual cocktail party chatter, a woman who was accustomed to being delightful, with bright blue eyes flashing and a red mouth that matched her tomato-red dress, cinched at the waist with an attractive patent leather belt, said she was feeling ostracized and pressured to conform to the *au naturelle* style of the group, and she'd spent her whole life conforming, and—goddammit—she was sick and tired of it. Joshua congratulated her on finding her own voice, and the woman looked confused, then beamed.

A woman who hadn't spoken for the first two months talked about feeling out of sync with the group because she was lame from childhood polio. Her whole life she'd felt different and like able-bodied people got all the perks. She'd never had a close relationship with a man, and she felt like everyone else got more attention from Joshua than she did.

Joshua listened, expressionless, then turned to Harmony and said, "Harmony, what would you say to that?"

Harmony felt adrenaline shoot through her stomach, and her mouth turned to cardboard. She was here to have energy sex with Joshua, not to be somebody's shrink.

"Well?" said Joshua. "Can you say something to Crystal?"

Crystal! Thank god he'd said her name. Although Harmony had spent three weekends with these people, she couldn't remember their names.

"Well, Crystal," she began, with no idea what she was going to say. "If you want more attention, maybe you need to talk. I've never heard you speak before. Also, I don't really know what perks you think everybody else is getting. Of course, I haven't had polio, but I wonder what you get out of believing everybody else is getting more than you are. Does that make you a martyr or something?"

Crystal turned crimson and several people reached to comfort her, glaring at Harmony.

Harmony felt their eye rays like daggers through her heart. What had she done? All she'd intended was to be silent and enjoy Joshua.

"She's right," announced Joshua, and the room did a communal gasp. "Crystal, you need to examine the negative pleasure you get out of seeing yourself as deprived. Now let's get out the tables. We're going to do healing in this morning's session. Crystal, I suggest you pair with Harmony, and you be the healer." Harmony and Crystal froze. "I've got to go to second year now. Have a great healing," he said and he left.

Harmony had taken the healer role in previous classes and didn't know what to expect as the healee to a healer who clearly loathed her. How dare Joshua make this so complicated? And, even worse, how dare he walk out? Well, maybe she could apologize and make it all go away. She approached Crystal and—womp!—it was like slamming into a wall made of hate. "Crystal," she said, afraid to breach the wall, "I'm really sorry. He took me by surprise, and I didn't know what I was saying."

Crystal glared at her with rattlesnake eyes. "Don't give me that. You knew exactly what you were saying. How about we just do this without a lot of conversation."

Harmony lay down on the table dreading the first touch. She watched Crystal limp to the foot end; someone lowered the lights; an assistant began giving directions; and the healing commenced.

Crystal's hands were icy, and Harmony contracted away from them. Somewhere around her fourth chakra—the heart—Harmony thought she was going to die. Crystal's hands felt knife-like, cold-slicing into her chest cavity. Harmony held her breath, and when she could tolerate it no more, she lurched off the table decking Crystal with her elbow.

"Ow!" yelled Crystal.

"I'm sorry," gasped Harmony. "I can't do this." And she ran to the bathroom.

She sat for a long time, counting her breaths. Once, somebody knocked on the stall door and asked if she was all right, and she said she was fine and would be out in a few minutes. By the time she came out, the class had broken for lunch. Harmony returned to the classroom and sank down against the wall to try to eat her brown-bag lunch, but it tasted like paper. So instead, she turned off the lights and lay on a mat. She was too wired to sleep, but she did dream. In an awake dream, she saw her hands break off, finger by finger. Then her feet and legs. "Don't be afraid," said a voice, and she saw that it was the ghostly being she'd met at Luanne's. Only this time it came as an animal, and it was eating bits of her hands. Horrified, Harmony watched as her rib cage split apart. I'm crazy, she thought. She was wide awake watching this thing reach for her face, when the door banged open and chatting, laughing students poured in.

"Hi, Harmony, are you feeling any better?" one asked, flicking on the lights.

Harmony checked to see where her legs were and found they were right where they belonged. Not only that, but the ghost animal was gone. "Huh?" she said, trying hard to sound sane.

"You should have come with us to lunch. We had Chinese."

In the next few minutes, everyone returned. An assistant sat where Joshua usually did and announced that they'd spend the afternoon discussing anything that might have come up during the morning session.

The gay guy said that he still wasn't pleased that Joshua was letting students teach, and the assistants smiled and nodded beneficently as they, too, had said such things back when they were neophytes. One assistant suggested the worrier just allow his feelings to be. One of the class members—a woman in her thirties who was getting her degree in psychology—suggested the worrier express his feelings by pounding a pillow with a baton that was used for this purpose. Everybody seemed to think that was a good idea, so they pulled all the big pillows into the middle of the circle and handed the baton to the guy. He studied the pillows, then announced that they were just pillows; he needed to direct his feelings at a person while he hit them. The lead assistant told him to choose a volunteer, and he looked around the circle and stopped at Harmony who was sitting cross-legged on her chair wondering how many minutes were left in this class and if her legs would fall off on the walk to the subway. Her stomach felt queasy and she was having trouble focusing.

"Harmony!" said the assistant for the second time.

"Huh?" said Harmony.

"Hank would like you to stand behind the pillows for this exercise."

"Who's Hank?" asked Harmony.

"That's all the motivation I need," said the gay guy and he began thwacking the pillows.

The next few minutes were a blackout for Harmony, and when she came to, she was crouched in a fetal position behind her chair. One of the assistants was touching her back and asking if she was all right. Realizing that she still had her arms and legs, she responded that she was fine and returned to her seat. The assistants looked at each other, shrugged, and began to continue, but the psychology student interrupted, suggesting they all take a break. Harmony thought this was an excellent idea, and as people milled around getting tea and chatting, she quietly gathered her coat and bag and left.

The air was cold when she hit the street. Winter was good. She liked a strong numbing wind in her face. She turned toward the subway, then decided to walk home instead.

It took more than an hour—although time was fuzzy so it was hard to tell—and by the time she crept into her apartment, her teeth were chattering and when she yanked at her gloves, she was afraid her fingers might come off. Her apartment was warm, overheated even. God bless overactive boilers. She inspected her plants; everybody looked okay. She started to look for Delilah under the bed, remembered, and fell to her knees sobbing. She cried until her eyes almost swelled shut, and then she thought of Kathy Smith. Kathy was always so understanding and encouraging. Kathy had known pain and loss, yet she always looked into the camera and assured Harmony that she could do it—just one more kick or leg lift or butt compression. Yes! *That* was the antidote. Harmony would turn on the video, jump up and down with Kathy, and then everything would be better.

"Heels up and down, and up and down," called Kathy from her pike—butt in the air—pose, and Harmony warmed up her thigh and calf muscles, only feeling a little light-headed. This was a good idea. Kathy would get her back to normal.

The arm exercises were fine. Harmony used three-pound weights, so she always went slower than the beat anyway. "*Feel* that bicep," ordered Kathy with a quick smile at the video students standing behind her. "Now triceps! People are always asking me, 'Kathy, how can we get at that loose skin?' Well, this is it, ladies! Feel the resistance!" Harmony pumped and felt the resistance, not quite in time with the music. If she fainted, at least she had carpeting with extra padding—installed after her downstairs neighbors had complained about all the jumping—so maybe it wouldn't hurt too much.

"All right!" said Kathy sweetly, twinkly-eyed and happy, swinging her hips and forearms, winding up for the aerobic portion of the workout. "Now let's get moving!"

Harmony tried. She really tried. But it was finally undeniable. It was during the "One-two-three-jumps," when she was jumping right and Kathy and the video class were jumping left, that Harmony realized she had not only lost her sense of rhythm, but her sense of space. "Step-kick! Step-kick! One-two-three, jump!" yelled Kathy. "Give it energy!" And Harmony crumbled.

"I can't, Kathy. I'm so sorry." she moaned, certain that Kathy was mad at her and would no longer be her friend and assure her that, even if she was dead tired and the burn was so extreme, she thought her legs might fall off, she could certainly do eight more kicks, or lifts, or bend-straightens, or leaps, and that, even though she was having a hard time, so did real athletes, and she was indeed a good person to be working out, and not to worry. Oh god, she could not do it, and if Kathy was so mad that she wouldn't come back on the TV the next time Harmony turned it on, she might as well give up.

With the TV blaring electronic aerobics music and Kathy yelling, "One-two-three-jump!" Harmony crawled into her bedroom, climbed into bed, and lay there in sweaty clothes and waited for night.

The next day, Sunday, Harmony knew there was someplace she was supposed to go, but since she couldn't remember where, it couldn't be too important. She turned off the TV. Why on earth had she left that on? She hated to squander electricity. The phone rang once, and she got so scared, she locked herself in the bathroom. After some time—she wasn't sure how long—she decided to take a bath. While she was soaking, the phone rang again. That phone was a monster! An electricity-guzzling monster! She held her breath and submerged. It occurred to her that if she opened her mouth and breathed in the water, she could go see Delilah and her parents. God, she missed Delilah.

"NO!" said the voice of her protector who had once yelled, "Hug!" And before she knew it, something had yanked her out of the water and she was toweling off.

She intended to disconnect the phone and put it in a closet, but before she did, she decided to make one call.

"Hello?" said Dr. Thompson.

"Oh, it's you!" said Harmony. "I was expecting a machine."

"Harmony?" said Dr. Thompson. She'd gotten home last night and wasn't due to resume sessions until next week. She'd dropped by the office to check mail and had picked up the phone on an impulse. "What's the matter? Are you all right?"

"Um," said Harmony. "I miss Delilah, and I'm afraid my legs are going to fall off. I couldn't even do one-two-three-jumps."

Dr. Thompson told Harmony to come right over—to take a cab.

Harmony couldn't remember the cab trip, but the next thing she knew, she was sitting on Dr. Thompson's beaten-up couch. Only this time, Dr. Thompson was on it too—holding her so her body wouldn't fall apart. Harmony had told Dr. Thompson about the girl with polio and the ghost animal that wanted to eat her face after her arms fell off. There was something about a guy wanting to beat her with a stick, but she wasn't sure if that was real. And Dr. Thompson just held her. Harmony didn't hear any thoughts because Dr. Thompson wasn't thinking. For the first time in thirty years, she just held someone and Sigmund Freud could go to hell.

Dr. Thompson had spent her last week of sabbatical at an alternative therapies conference where speakers included everyone from neuroscientists who mapped God in people's brains, to yoga masters who talked about the healing ability of the kundalini or "snake energy" coiled at the base of the spine, to shamans from Africa and South America. The shamans had described something called dismemberment visions where their bodies fell apart and were eaten by powerful healing animals. Although it went against all her psychotherapeutic training, Dr. Thompson was having a very strong impulse to deal with Harmony's obvious psychosis as if it were a shaman's vision.

"Harmony, I'd like to try something. Can you sit up?"

Harmony suddenly realized she was clinging to Dr. Thompson. How embarrassing. "Sure," she answered and shakily pushed herself upright.

"I'm going to sit on my chair now, okay?"

"Okay, that's fine," said Harmony, wondering how long she'd been here.

Dr. Thompson straightened her blouse and sat opposite Harmony. "There's nothing to be embarrassed about, although I'm glad you're feeling well enough to feel embarrassed now. Can you plant your feet on the ground and look into my eyes?"

Harmony had never been big on eye contact, but she made her best effort. Dr. T had nice eyes. They didn't dig into you like the girl with polio or the gay guy.

"I'd like you to try to listen to the sound of your own heartbeat now. Can you do that for me?"

Harmony nodded, felt around for the feeling of her heart, and was surprised to find it was still there. Faint at first, but the more she listened, the stronger it got: *ka-chung, ka-ka-chung*. And she could swear she heard the sloshing of blood. She watched Dr. Thompson's soft, steady eyes and she felt safe. *Ka-chung, ka-ka-chung*.

"Now imagine that beat is your whole body."

And Harmony felt it—her whole body throbbing, the whoosh of her blood coursing through it. *Ka-chung, ka-ka-chung*. Her sense of rhythm had returned.

"Now extend that feeling out of your body to me, to the whole room."

"Oh my god." Harmony teared up as a golden light lit up Dr. Thompson and the whole room throbbed.

"Now imagine that feeling extending to the whole building and out to the whole city."

Harmony had never felt so alive. And by the time she extended the beat to the country, something very peculiar had happened. She had turned into an enormous black woman standing in the middle of a waving yellow wheat field. She could see Dr. Thompson and hear her voice, but she was also someone else, somewhere else. And when Dr. Thompson told her to imagine her heartbeat encompassing the planet, the most extraordinary thing happened: Harmony lifted up her grass skirts, and squatting, gave birth to a huge pulsating green and blue liquid earth. She was on the earth but she was also birthing it. "Oh my god!" she screamed, tears streaming, and Dr. Thompson didn't need to be told: it was good.

The earth turned and pulsated, the tall grass waved, the oceans swirled, and Harmony, the huge black woman, stood twenty-five feet tall on great flat feet the size of lakes, and she twisted and undulated, her enormous hands spreading across the sky like giant, blue-black eagles in full flight, and as dusk came, she opened her dripping wet mouth, drew back her purplish tongue and howled. She howled like a wolf for its pack.

"What is it—who is it you want, sweetie?" asked Dr. Thompson touching her hand.

And Harmony deflated. "I- I- I-. I just want my tribe."

And although it went against everything in her training and she didn't really understand what had just happened, Dr. Thompson knew Harmony was all right, so she didn't recommend drugs or suggest a hospital stay. Instead, she asked Harmony to see her several times in the coming weeks, and if the fee was a problem, they could work something out.

Harmony thought this was a good idea, and since she was in a slow period at work, she took two weeks of her vacation time.

Over the next weeks, Dr. Thompson read everything she could get her hands on about black goddesses, African creation myths, and shaman initiations. She felt curious and alive and excited and hopeful in a way she hadn't since her first marriage. Yes, she had refueled on the sabbatical, and now, although she didn't altogether understand what was happening with Harmony, she was certain it was good.

Chapter 18

SOLILOQUY

Joshua had no knowledge of a problem until he read the first letter:

Dear Joshua,

Your assistants are incompetent. I'm better now after two weeks of intensive therapy, but I want you to know that you are inviting disaster by having students with no psychological training doing unsupervised therapy with other students. I am a very strong person and have bounced back from the breakdown I suffered during our last class, but I feel it is my obligation to warn you that had it happened to somebody with a more fragile constitution, you would likely have had a suicide on your hands.

My therapist has suggested I return for another weekend before I make up my mind about quitting the school. I enjoy being around you, but your irresponsible teaching practices are enabling and creating a dangerous environment ruled by feckless quacks. I'll see you next month.

Sincerely yours,
Harmony Rogers

"What the hell happened?" he demanded at the emergency meeting of the entire assistants' group. It was a huge gathering, including many who had not attended Harmony's class, and everyone looked blank.

"I know she seemed upset during the pillows exercise," said Martha, who'd been lead assistant in the class, "but I didn't know there was a problem. She seemed all right when she left."

"She left?!" gasped Joshua. He was livid. "Why didn't anyone tell me she left?"

"I just did," said Martha, starting to cry. Joshua had never yelled at her before. Several other assistants said that they had suspected something was up, but they were afraid to trust their instincts.

Joshua said if there was ever a question, they should call him.

One of the assistants, who said he hadn't been in the class, asked how come Joshua didn't "know" there was a problem without being called, and Joshua ignored the question and apologized to Martha, giving her an extra warm hug until she stopped crying and said she loved him.

Joshua said this was a learning experience for everybody, but from now on if there was a problem, he should be called—no matter how busy he was. Then he left the room.

The assistants looked at each other. "What just happened?" asked the one who'd challenged Joshua's omniscience—he was one of the three straight men in the school, and a look passed between him and the other two. Another student said she felt upset, but she didn't know why. A few had funny feelings, but didn't say anything because they were probably just imagining things. After all, everyone knew what a gifted healer Joshua was, how generous and loving. Why, he could never say no. No matter how much else he had to do, when they needed him, he was there. He sacrificed family time for his work. As he said, it was his destiny. Joshua Gardner was one in a million and it was an honor to volunteer at his school.

The second letter was stronger:

Dear Joshua,

There were some things I couldn't remember when I wrote my first letter. My therapist explained that you can temporarily lose memories when your "circuits are blown" due to trauma—which I think I experienced during the table work. Anyway, since I've settled down, my memory of the entire episode has returned.

I was very upset by the table work. I don't know why you paired Crystal and me when you knew how angry she was at me. I was so upset I hallucinated during the break and was completely dissociated when we began the afternoon session. Had there been an experienced professional in charge, perhaps he or she would have noticed. As it was, my upset was not only missed, but I was told to act as the focus for Hank's rage. I could barely remember my own name, let alone his, and this enraged him. I was told to stand behind the pillows so he could focus on me while he thwacked them with a baton. I found the experience absolutely terrifying, but when I protested, I was told, and I quote: "The work at this school is to become aware of our habitual bad patterns and to make another choice." I was told that my isolation and aloofness had alienated the rest of the class, so it was important that I now choose to participate by standing there while Hank beat the crap out of a pillow.

My therapist is of the opinion that this event on top of my earlier trauma and dissociation brought me close to a nervous breakdown.

I hope if you cannot be present in classes in the future, you will assign them to experienced professional teachers.

Sincerely yours,
Harmony Rogers

The third letter was brief:

Dear Joshua,

I have decided to quit the school after next month's weekend. I would appreciate a refund of the balance of my tuition ready for me at that time. I appreciate your powerful energy and ability to thought-talk, but this school is not right for me.

Sincerely yours,
Harmony Rogers

Chapter 19

WATCHING

Harmony had heard there was a community garden on Avenue B. Probably it would be closed and brown on a cold February weekend, but she had never done Dr. T's assignment to investigate garden clubs and she could use a walk. She dressed in layers—a black L.L. Bean parka over mismatched sweatshirts and jeans over long underwear—and pushed her hair up under a pilling green and yellow stocking cap; she really needed to get a professional haircut one of these days. As she exited her building, she briefly considered heading west to the bookstore to browse some more psychology books, but she'd committed to carrying out Dr. T's assignment. It was the least she could do after all those extra sessions; it was on her to-do list, and Harmony was diligent about order and commitments.

Even in the frigid weather, Broome Street was abustle. She passed the plumbing supplies delivery truck, the Italian restaurant, the Pan-Asian vegetarian store, the Filipino chapel, the Vietnamese restaurant, Engine 55 firehouse, and Holy Trinity Ukrainian Orthodox Cathedral. Harmony loved her diverse neighborhood; it made her feel almost normal. She assumed that most people assumed she was not white, but they never asked.

On Chrystie Street, she turned north and strolled up through the lighting district, cut through barren Roosevelt Park, and headed east on bleak Delancey. If she was going to join this community garden, maybe even have a plot, just watering would require a substantial hike; ah, that could be her excuse for not doing it!

On impulse, she turned left on Orchard: hats and the world's largest selection of gloves displayed in shops owned by people named Giuseppe and Cellini were always a cheerer-upper. And nothing bad could happen on a block run by old Italian men. On East Houston, she turned east to Avenue B. The garden was just six more blocks—opposite a monolithic red brick building called the Earth School.

Nice, thought Harmony, squinting through an iron fence at the barren quarter acre of garden plots, plastic-covered mounds, and bare trees. The gate was chain-locked, but there were a few people engrossed in some kind of work: a skinny white string-bean of a girl with long bangs; a potato-shaped black woman with a shovel in one hand and a cigarette in the other who seemed to be supervising from her post atop a stage-like structure at the back of the garden; a sweet-faced girl in her early twenties with long, blonde hair and a lithe dancer's way of moving; a loud speech-teacher–type woman who was lecturing a surly young man, flamboyant in red and purple with a tattooed neck; a woman with a severe curvature of the spine and pronounced wobble who limped back and forth from her plot to a shed behind the stage; and a huge woman with braids who Harmony could have sworn was Luanne Carpenter.

A familiar group. Spooky.

Perhaps she'd try again in the spring.

Although she doubted that there were any more straight men in this community garden than there were in the parallel universe of healing school, Harmony still thought she should eschew hasty judgments and instead heed Dr. T's advice and stay open to possibilities.

During her cold walk home, she reflected on the importance of men. She missed energy sex since her falling out with Joshua. How could someone as aware as he be so obtuse? she wondered as she turned west on Houston. How could he not see his assistants were neophytes? Half of them were so in love with him they had ceased to think critically, and none of them had any business teaching classes, she thought, grinding her teeth as she headed south on Chrystie. Harmony was still shaky from her near-breakdown. She blamed Joshua for creating the situation; but she missed their subtle meetings, the heat in her uterus, thought-talking at night. She missed the very first member of her tribe that she had ever met, she thought as she headed home on Broome.

Harmony loved her sessions with Dr. Thompson, but, even with insurance reimbursements, they were expensive, and since she had opted to pay healing school tuition in full rather than talk out loud about money with Joshua—the thought of which made her skin crawl, for reasons she did not understand—she was looking forward to her refund from the school. She unlocked her building door, and trudging up the stairs, once again, wondered if she should get a cat.

***

The night before class, Harmony had a dream: She and Joshua were facing each other. Their energetic bodies merged, making love. She moved closer, opening her mouth to kiss him, hungry for his soft lips, but at the last second, he threw up a wall—smack to the whole front of her body.

"Why not?!" she yelled, but he just backed away. "Why not?" Then she was falling backwards through the floors of the building. And when she hit bottom, she was in the Pan-Asian vegetarian store lying on Dr. Thompson's couch. "Why not?" she wailed. "Why not?"

Harmony arrived half an hour early to her fifth weekend of healing school and was told by the assistant at reception that first year would be in the main room. People were usually late, which was fine by her. She had brought coffee and expected to make herself comfortable on a mat in a corner before everybody began drifting in.

As she opened the door, fifty pairs of eyes fastened on her. "Gee, I'm sorry; I didn't mean to—" Harmony backed out.

"No, no," called Joshua. "Come in. We just had an assistants' meeting, but we're done." He gathered some papers on a clipboard and left by the little door behind the sound system. Many of the assistants stood and stretched with self-conscious nonchalance. Harmony didn't recognize most of them because they hadn't attended her classes. But in one sudden telepathic jolt, she knew why they were all here: to observe her. She knew Joshua had read her letters and sent out the word, and everyone had come to learn. On one hand, this was flattering and she felt like a movie star. On the other, she felt like a really pissed-off lab rat. The stupid idiots, why didn't they already know how to recognize trauma? They'd done three and four years of school, and some were working in private practices. Why hadn't they covered this already? She found a place to curl up with her coffee, and she tried to ignore the energetic tentacles aimed at her from all directions—probing, examining. Fuck them all. She'd be out of here as soon as she got her refund, and

Joshua could go to hell.

"How are you doing?"

It was a familiar voice. Harmony looked up to see Grace coming toward her. "Hi," she said, surprised.

"I haven't seen you at work. Is everything all right?"

How do you answer a person who asks a question she already knows the answer to because she not only is sleeping with the source of the answer, but has been fully briefed in a secret meeting? Harmony didn't answer.

Grace looked baffled. "I hope you don't mind my coming this weekend," she continued.

Harmony shrugged and gestured to the crowd. "It looks like a big weekend."

"Maybe so," said Grace. "Well . . . I'm going to get tea. Can I get you anything?"

Harmony toasted with her coffee and watched her walk away. Without looking, she could feel the eyes of several students following her every move.

Sometimes, if you listen very big, you can hear conversations that have taken place at other times. It has to do with focus. If you understand that there is no sequential time but just a big soup of events, you can then observe anything simply by expanding your mind like hot air, and then focusing on what you want to hear. Harmony had learned this when she wondered why her first grade teacher was so pretend-nice to her, but just regular with the other kids. The day she first wondered, she was standing on the edge of a blacktop behind a school that looked very much like the Earth School on Avenue B. As she watched the other kids chase each other around the playground, she felt Mrs. Brady's drill-like eyes watching her, and in her mind, she wondered why. And suddenly she heard this conversation:

> "They found her in a box in a locked closet. Can you imagine doing that to your baby?" said Mrs. Brady.
>
> "They said she didn't make any noise for the first eight months after the adoption. Can you imagine bringing that kind of trouble into your family? She'll never be right," said someone else.

"Well, they had no choice at their age. They were lucky to get any child. I say, God bless them."

"Of course, of course. God bless them. It's got to be difficult though."

So that's why I like closets, thought six-year-old Harmony, watching Mrs. Brady watching her watching the regular kids.

What's most amazing about people watching you is that they think it is a one-way action. Harmony drank her coffee knowing the fifty pairs of eyes drilling into her had no idea she was observing them back. Like Mrs. Brady, they made two false assumptions: that she was a "thing" to be watched; and that you could only see out of your eyeballs and hear out of your ears. Harmony had eyeballs and ears all over her body. So did Joshua. It was why she loved him.

"She is completely open," he had said to the assistants in the briefing meeting a few minutes ago. "You have to work more gently with somebody like this. A little goes a long way. And be careful. She misses nothing."— Harmony heard these comments as she drank her coffee and listened with her big mind. And she knew the assistants had no idea what Joshua was telling them. But he knew. Because he was the same. And the thought of getting her refund and never seeing him again, the loss of the one person who thought-talked faster than the speed of light—the prospect of that loneliness made her heart hurt.

"Then don't do it," said Joshua.

Without turning, Harmony knew he was standing five feet behind her, smiling. "You leave me no choice," she answered. "You've created a dangerous situation."

"Why is that bad?" asked Joshua. "You've always got a choice." And he walked away.

Joshua told the class that this weekend they'd be doing less talk and more experiential work. They paired for an exercise where they stared into each other's eyes which made Harmony's eyeballs spastic. Then they took turns falling backwards into each other's arms—which turned out to be a warm-up for the main event:

The room got very quiet as the first student, the 200-pound potato woman whose name was Sherry, mounted the table and stood backwards on the edge. Below her, two seated rows of students faced each other with locked arms forming a catching net. Sherry was terrified; so were the catchers. What if they couldn't hold her and she broke her back?

"Don't worry. There are enough of you, and the physics of weight distribution will take care of things," Joshua assured them.

Harmony wasn't in this catching group, and she was glad.

The woman looked like a piano dropping when she finally went, and there was a communal exhale as she hit the arms. Joshua was right. She landed safely, and they gently lowered her to the mat.

"Everybody, pull your hands away very slowly at the same time," said Joshua softly. "Watch each other. Work as a unit. Sherry, you stay put. Enjoy the sensations."

Sherry, who normally had a face like a prune, turned angelic as she lay with closed eyes, enjoying something mysterious, but obviously pleasurable.

"Who's next?" asked Joshua after Sherry finally sat up.

Hank was tense and mean, attempting to direct the catchers which was not possible. Joshua waited out his ranting and patiently said, "Whenever you're ready, Hank." Hank, dressed in purple cargo pants with a red V-neck T-shirt that revealed part of a small rose tattoo creeping up over his collar bone, posed with his heels off the edge of the table as if he were about to back dive. He took a deep breath, but instead of dropping, erupted in more instructions. "No," groaned the catchers. A couple of students complained that their arms were aching from the tension of holding them outstretched for so long. "For god's sake, just fall!" squeaked a normally soft-spoken girl named Clementine, and everybody laughed. Incensed, Hank took a breath and fell.

As he hit, his body broke at the waist and knees as if he were having second thoughts, and the impact almost broke the net of arms. Harmony made a mental note to fall flat like a board—relaxed but flat. Once lowered to the ground, Hank blushed and a sickly smile contorted his mouth as he got an erection. Then his body let loose a horrible mildew odor. Harmony clamped a hand over her nose and looked around, but nobody else reacted. Well, maybe that was good—maybe that meant they wouldn't smell her when she let loose.

"Harmony, you're up," said Joshua, shooting her a flirtatious grin, but Harmony ignored him. She mounted the table, ignoring the assistants' helping hands. She surveyed the catchers, nodded acknowledgement, turned her back, and dropped. She looked like a tree falling as she pivoted back on stiff feet and fell in a piece.

The room gasped. It was a holy moment, an act of naked faith, a body holding nothing back. It was so easy. Harmony trusted falling. She trusted dying. It was living that could be dangerous.

The group caught her like a newborn dropping out of a sky womb. Gently they lowered her to the mat, and without direction, withdrew their hands in one motion. Joshua nodded approval and held a finger to his lips for silence.

Harmony's heart felt like warm molasses spreading up and down her body. Her face flushed; her arms, fingers, ribs, and pelvis filled, and down and down. As the heat pooled in her crotch, her limbs began to vibrate. But she was not self-conscious. No longer could she feel the probing eyes because they were nothing different from her—there was no them, no her. No cage. Only hot, soothing energy.

After a time, the vibrating abated, and she opened her eyes and looked up into the faces of her catchers. "Thank you," she whispered, opening her arms. And in one motion, they fell on her, hugging, holding, whimpering.

After a time, they let each other go. Harmony, suddenly feeling embarrassed, picked herself up and joined the group as a catcher while another person mounted the table. And the falling and catching continued.

Joshua was having a hard time. Watching Harmony was like seeing Emily being born . . . only different. He whispered to one of the assistants and left the room.

When he'd built the school, Joshua had constructed a private bathroom with a locked door hidden behind a sliding wall, so many of the students didn't even know it was there.

"Get it together, Josh," he said out loud as he gripped the sink in his hidden room. His stomach was vibrating so fast he felt nauseous, and he could taste his heart. He couldn't say what it was—the way she fell, the total surrender? He'd never been able to let go that way in his life, but he wasn't jealous. No, he was in awe. Shit! Stop this. He had a wife and baby and a school to run. He was a good man, even if he did have a girlfriend. After all, he'd refused to kiss Harmony in their dream meeting last night. At the last minute, he'd done the right thing and thrown up the wall. He remembered his nursing fantasy—the way she'd gone along with it, exposing her beautiful breasts and allowing her milk to— No, stop this! Do not screw with Harmony!

He needed to keep things together, and Harmony was trouble. So direct, yet unpredictable. He'd never met anybody like her, except— He caught his reflection in the mirror in the hidden room. No, he wouldn't say it. He was fine being one of a kind. Just fine. He threw cold water on his face and returned to his class.

After everyone had fallen off the table as well as caught, Roger, the assistant in charge, had told them to lie down and contemplate their experience. When Joshua got back, the lights were off; bodies were spread across the floor like a killing field after a battle; Bach's Cello *Suite No. 1 in G Major* was flooding the room through the sound system; and several people were weeping.

In the far corner was a ball of bright red-orange energy spouting up from a red-orange geyser, pulsating in time to the music. Joshua saw it and, knowing he should stay put, he moved toward it. It's just that she presented a challenge.

"We can't do this," thought-talked Harmony, feeling his approach.

But this only made Joshua want her more. Her eyes were closed, but he knew she knew he was there, standing over her, his legs straddling her body. The lights were off; nobody could see. She opened her eyes and looked into his. "Do you want me to do it?" he thought-talked. And she nodded.

Years ago, Joshua had discovered his marksmanship with energy. All it took was a thought, a clear intention, and out shot a streamer. He could aim it like a laser beam from any part of his body, hitting a target with the accuracy and the focus of a master.

"Are you sure?" he thought-asked.

"Yes," she thought-answered.

And a red-orange streamer shot out of his pelvis penetrating the pulsating ball spouting out of Harmony's. Her eyes rolled back in her head and she thought-roared so loud it was a miracle the room didn't explode. "Oh my god," she thought-moaned.

He smiled. And as he started to unstraddle her, she curled around his ankle like a kitten. "No, no, don't go," she thought-begged.

And he knew she would make love to him right there in the middle of the room if he were willing. *Score*! He smiled and walked away.

Harmony didn't care who was looking. Let them think what they liked. She was no longer alone. She was down off the pole, out of the cage of preconceptions and expectations. She had no idea what could or might happen, and she liked not knowing. She told the assistant Martha that she'd decide about quitting next month, so hold onto the refund check.

Martha said okay, even though she had no check and no idea what Harmony was talking about, since Joshua had given no order for a refund.

Joshua had planned an after-class date with Grace, so he called Judy to say first year was running late and she shouldn't wait up; he'd grab a bite and maybe meet Frederic for a movie and a drink, and he'd see her in the morning.

Chapter 20

DISCONNECTED

Harmony looked at the pile of submissions falling off her chair and desktop. For two weeks, she hadn't thought about Joseph or her job. She imagined sending an email that said simply, "I quit." When she was in her twenties, if a job got too boring or the people too annoying, she left, which was why she had such a checkered resume, which was why she was lucky to have this job—which made her even more resentful.

Resentment! That was Hank's mildew smell. Harmony closed her eyes and tried to smell herself, but it was useless. She imagined she must stink as much as everyone else. Bummer. But at least now she knew the smells, the energy, the whole thing was real. Although she'd lived in this world of "other senses," she'd always had a secret doubt: What if she were imagining it all? What if she were crazy? But after energetic love with Joshua, those doubts evaporated. And Joshua healed with the energy. Harmony had never thought of herself as a "people person," but maybe she could help too. Maybe there was even a new job in it that was better than a plant store; after all, Joshua seemed to have no problems making a living. And healing people would certainly be more interesting than perpetual tidying.

"Good morning, Harmony, did you have a good vacation?"

It was Cora. Reflexively, Harmony took a deep breath through her mouth. When Joshua had zapped her with his energy, she'd felt alive. Roxana had said her experience on the healing table had been one of the best she'd ever had. It was lonely keeping people away all the time, and this job was so boring. The community garden was dreary, and Dr. Thompson had encouraged her to find friends. Suddenly, she remembered how she felt as the African earth mother. "Hi, Cora, my vacation was great. I got a lot of rest. How are you? Are you feeling better? What's going on?"

Cora took a step back and wondered if Harmony was on drugs. "You got a lot of mail. I tried to keep it neat, but it fell over."

"No problem," said Harmony, smiling and making eye contact. "It's probably all the earthquakes." Cora looked puzzled. "In India . . . and El Salvador." Harmony had been memorizing the TV news in an attempt to be connected to the world. "I was making a joke. So how are you feeling? You must be relieved the chemo is over. I can't smell anything."

Cora touched her wig and looked at her peculiarly. "Some of us make it a habit to wear deodorant."

"Of course, of course," said Harmony. "I meant you smell good. Is that a new perfume?"

Cora frowned. "I don't wear perfume. I've got allergies."

"Of course, of course, I'm sorry. So how are you feeling?" Harmony softened the front of her body to feel for Cora's tumor. It felt like a dime-sized hard spot embedded deep in her left side. Harmony remembered how Joshua zapped her, and decided to try it. She focused her energy in her own left midsection and thought of sending out a streamer to destroy the tumor, and instantly, a blast shot out of her into Cora's stomach.

Cora shuddered and grabbed her midsection. "Listen, I just wanted to tell you Joseph is going to be late this morning, but he wants to make sure all the contracts are done for March. Boy, I don't feel so good." And she bee-lined for the ladies' room.

Harmony smiled. She was going to zap that tumor into oblivion, and Cora would never even know about it. She laughed and began sorting through the toppling piles of mail.

Cora bent over the toilet and retched. She hadn't felt this sick since the third day following chemo. She threw up until there was nothing but bile, and when the bile was gone, blood. She knew it was from the strain of the spasms, so she wasn't alarmed; she could ask about it at her checkup tomorrow. She washed her face, reapplied her makeup, straightened the damned wig, and went back to her cubicle.

"I was thinking maybe you and Grace and I could have lunch today," called Harmony cheerfully.

Cora had never seen Harmony drink alcohol, but maybe she'd developed a problem over vacation.

"We could go to the cafeteria. What do you think?" Harmony knew Cora didn't like her, but Joshua said the way to love is through love. After all, it had worked on a hard ass like her.

"Can we talk about it later?" said Cora. "I'm not in a food mood right now." She could still taste vomit.

"Sure, that would be fine. I'll call Grace, if you don't mind."

"Whatever," answered Cora. She knew Harmony was seeing a shrink. Maybe it was a new prescription. Cora had heard there were drugs that could make you more sociable, but this was obnoxious.

When Joseph arrived, Harmony greeted him with a smile and a pile of contracts in alphabetical order. She told him the March issue was coming along nicely and complimented him on the December issue with the rescued houseplant piece.

Joseph eyed her suspiciously and said he was glad she liked December. He just knew she had found a new job and would be giving notice, throwing his whole life topsy-turvy because he'd just booked a trip to the Bahamas with his lover from accounting. Damn that woman! The tickets were specially discounted and nonrefundable.

Harmony genuinely liked Grace. She knew she had been stand-offish when they'd seen each other at school, and she thought if they could have an easy lunch, maybe things would feel more comfortable the next time they met there. "Hi, Grace, it's Harmony. I was wondering if you'd like to have lunch. Cora might come too. Call me back as soon as you get this message. Oh, it was good to see you this weekend."

Harmony decided to try to work on Cora through the cubicle wall, so as she emailed rejections, she visualized sending laser beams into the wad of cancer cells in Cora's stomach.

At twelve o'clock, Cora told Harmony she was sorry, but she'd have to take a rain check on lunch, and she went home sick.

Harmony smiled. Joshua said people always felt worse as things got better. You have to fully experience pain before you can discard it. Harmony knew that Cora's tumor was screaming for dear life, knowing its days were numbered.

Grace called to say she was too busy to have lunch, but maybe another time.

Harmony wondered how much you could charge for a healing session and how you acquired clients. She wondered how long it would take to have enough regular income to quit this job. And did you have to like everyone who came to you, or would the energy mojo work no matter what you felt? She wasn't that crazy about having strangers in her apartment, and she wondered how much an office might cost.

"Tell me again, exactly what did he do?" asked Dr. Thompson. She'd heard what Harmony had said, but something did not sit right. Harmony's sudden brightness was attractive, but empty.

"Okay. It was like this: I was lying on the floor filled with sexy feelings after the falling exercise, and he came into the room. I always know when he comes in because there's an energy surge. Anyway, I could feel him heading for me, and I suddenly thought about his wife, who is probably like Hillary Rodham Clinton who I like a lot, and how, even if we weren't technically having an affair, this was so mean and I should just get my refund and get out of there. So I thought-talked to him that we shouldn't do this. I don't know—maybe I was just getting myself off the hook responsibility-wise, because he kept coming and I was glad. He stood over me—"

"Excuse me," interrupted Dr. Thompson, "exactly how did he stand over you?"

"You know—with one foot on either side of my body."

Dr. Thompson nodded. "Go on."

"I opened my eyes and he was smiling at me. Really sexy. Then he thought-asked, 'Do you want me to do it?' And I knew he meant touch me in the second chakra—that's where your uterus is, and it feels unbelievably sexy—and I answered, 'Yes,' and he did it, and it was the most amazing thing I've ever felt. So I decided not to quit the school just yet. Not only that, but then I thought maybe I could help people with my energy sensibilities since I can do a lot of the same stuff he does and it probably pays much better than a plant store. So I've been zapping Cora's tumor all day. I think it's working because she went home sick. I'm out of the cage of my own expectations!

Oh, and by the way, the community garden thing was a bust. But it doesn't matter because it's all the same people as healing school. Interchangeable. Amazing, huh?"

Dr. Thompson pursed her lips and thought. "Can I ask you a question, Harmony?" she said after a long pause.

"Of course," said Harmony. "Please."

"What are you feeling right now in your body?"

Harmony looked at her body, puzzled. "Not much," she answered and felt some more. "Absolutely nothing. No missile. How peculiar. Maybe I'm cured."

"Have you been jumping with Kathy Smith?"

"No. I forgot all about that. I haven't jumped since before the last class. Weird, huh?"

"Can you look at me?" asked Dr. Thompson gently. "Look at me the way you did when we did the heartbeat exercise."

Harmony obliged, and for no reason she understood, a huge ball of tears welled up in her throat and she felt like sobbing. Maybe it was that Dr. T had such nice eyes that it broke her heart.

"Why are you fighting it?" asked Dr. Thompson. "What would be wrong with crying?"

Harmony was having trouble breathing, and then all of a sudden her whole body was sobbing, and she had no idea why.

"You know what, Harmony?" said Dr. Thompson, handing her the Kleenex box.

"No, I don't know what," said Harmony, blowing her nose. She'd been so happy when she'd come in, and now she was going to walk out of here with ugly, red, swollen eyes and guilt about having abandoned Kathy Smith.

"Sometimes, when you really see another human being, it can make you cry."

And for some reason, this brought on a whole new round of sobbing. Dr. Thompson said Harmony was her last patient, so she could take as much time in the waiting room as she needed to collect herself. She said not to worry—the door to the office would lock automatically when she left.

Chapter 21

MIRROR, MIRROR

Many years ago, Harmony had found a full-length, snakewood-framed mirror, along with several houseplants, on the street in someone's trash. She'd easily bagged the little plants in her tote, but the mirror weighed a ton. She didn't particularly want a mirror, but the wood was stunning with its wormy rill grain and, even with the discolored patches on the glass, this one would create a secondary light source for her plants. She lugged it two blocks, then up four flights, and never got around to hanging it or even figuring out the best placement to reflect her obstructed southern sunlight. For ten years it had leaned against the dark wall in between her bureau with the water garden and her closet.

When she got home from therapy, she decided it was time she tried to see—really see—herself. She closed the curtains in the living room, turned on the big floor lamp and all the full-spectrum plant lamps. Then she took off her blouse, her pants, her underwear, and even her socks, laid them neatly over her desk chair, and went into the bedroom.

The mirror was even heavier and more unwieldy than she remembered and, as she struggled with it against her chest, she wished she had waited to disrobe. Why was she always doing things backwards?

Where to put it? The darkest place was the corner of the east wall that caught a bright sliver of building-reflected western sun for about twenty minutes in summer, just before dusk. If she placed the mirror there, she could double that light and give the *dracaenas* an end-of-day treat.

Squashing the mirror against her breasts, she half-dragged, half-carried it to the spot, then pushed and slid it against the dark wall. Great. She should have done this ten years ago. If only— Oh god! She startled at the movement in the corner and, for an insane moment, believed a naked woman had been hiding in her living room.

"I'm out of my mind." She bent over to get the blood back into her head.

Okay, enough of that. Dr. T had said that if you really see a person, it can make you cry, so before doing this experiment, Harmony made sure she had a box of tissues on hand.

She was excited. Although she never would have admitted it, at a deep level, she had no idea what she looked like. Of course, she had seen herself—in the bathroom mirror when she brushed her teeth and put on mascara. But she saw parts—teeth, eyelashes—for the purpose of completing a necessary task. She ordered clothes from L.L.Bean and glanced at them on her for fit. She had so little idea of what she looked like as a whole person that when she saw herself in the annual company photo, she had a moment of profound disorientation.

"I am going to do this," she said to nobody. And she purposefully stepped back from the mirror just enough so that her whole naked body was in the frame.

Where to begin?

Her feet were nice. Well shaped with a slight Morton's toe, clean toe nails. Legs okay, although she could lose a few pounds in the thighs. She'd double her leg lifts with Kathy Smith. Crotch—yup. Tummy—not flat. Hips—ditto to the thighs. Breasts were there just the way she remembered them. Everything was in the right place.

The problem came at her face. As she snuck a look, she noticed that her left eye was rolled out to the left side. Turkey vision. Poor binocular vision and depth perception. She blinked and it shifted into alignment with the right one. She'd always had a lazy eye, which never focused or took in enough light, but the pediatrician had explained to her parents that, although this might affect depth perception, people lived their whole lives seeing quite adequately with one eye. Still, Harmony was startled to witness, with her good eye, the lazy eye pointing in the wrong direction.

"Focus pocus!" she directed her reflection. "I want to really see me." She grabbed a tissue in preparation . . .

Nothing. Not only did no strong emotion come, but the more Harmony stared at her face, the fuzzier it became, until she could have sworn her good right eye was getting as impaired as the lazy left one. "Damn!" she barked, blinking hard. For a nanosecond after the blink, she could have sworn she saw the clear image of a strange-looking, wide-eyed, oval-faced gypsy girl, but almost the instant it became clear, it faded into fuzz, rubbed out by the dark shadows floating around and through it, blurring her features.

"Well, maybe I'm not a narcissist after all," she said with a shrug.

Chapter 22

JOSHUA AND GRACE

Even though Joshua had abandoned construction work for teaching, when Frederic needed help, he was happy to oblige.

"So how much is this gonna cost me?" asked Frederic, grinning.

Joshua swiped him playfully. "Get outa here, old man. And tell me where you want these." He eyed the cement blocks piled six feet high against the kitchen wall. "I'm getting too old for pack animal work." Grace was meeting him here at five, and he wanted to have time to clean up.

"As soon as it gets warmer, I want to build a wall to block the jerk who shares the terrace." Frederic pointed out the kitchen window to the barren penthouse roof that he'd been intending to fix up for the last twenty-five years. "I'm finally gonna make a garden, and I don't want his mutt peeing all over it."

"Okay," said Joshua, squeezing his eyes shut and concentrating dramatically.

"What're you doing?" said Frederic.

"Telepathically ordering the over-soul of all canines to keep the guy's mutt off your side of the roof."

"You're so full of crap." Frederic took a deep drag on his cigarette, then exhaled, squinting at Joshua through the smoke. "I can't live with this crap in the kitchen. Let's take it outside. We can pile it against the water shed and put a tarp over it."

"We?" said Joshua, hoisting the first block. "Open the damn door."

Frederic laughed and flung open the reinforced metal door, letting in a shock of cold air. Joshua pretended to be overwhelmed by the weight as he lugged block after block out to the middle of the roof. Joshua had surprising strength for a man his size. You'd never guess it to look at him. He was nicely built, but hardly a muscle man. The strength came from sheer will. He just knew he could do things. He always had. And it didn't bother him to also know that these blocks would never move from their place under the tarp. This job had nothing to do with real construction. It was about Frederic knowing he had a friend who would lug his cement. Frederic had never married and had no family. And although Frederic never said it, Joshua knew he was afraid of dying alone.

"You're a wild man, Josh," said Frederic, lighting a new butt with the stub of the old one.

Joshua laughed and touched his heart, even though he knew it would make Frederic uncomfortable. Sometimes you have to make people uncomfortable. It was his job.

Frederic scowled and turned, pretending to examine the floor where the cement had been stacked, but really to hide. It only took a second, but when he saw Joshua seeing him, it made him cry. Frederic hadn't cried in fifty-seven years—since the day his mother died and all the softness went out of his life because he'd vowed never to risk that hurt again.

"So what time is your sweetheart getting here?" asked Frederic, busying himself with a broom and dustpan.

Joshua checked his watch. "Jeez. Now." He yanked off his dust-covered T-shirt and rummaged through his gym bag for the clean one.

"So howzat going?" asked Frederic, back in the role of father figure. "Does your wife know?"

Joshua shrugged and stuffed the soiled shirt into the bag. "You know I care about her. It's just—"

Frederic batted the air. "You don't have to explain. It's like old gym shorts."

"Come again?" Joshua loved the way Frederic surprised him.

"When gym shorts are new, the elastic is nice and snappy, and you think these are the perfect shorts. But sometimes the elastic just dies. There's no snap; they go slack. And when the elastic dies, there's no getting it back."

"You're a friggin' poet, Fred. Mind if I use the can?"

"There's new soap on the shelf above the tub," said Frederic, dumping the cement dust into the garbage.

Grace was used to male attention. She was a beautiful woman and comfortable with it. Even as a child, she had understood men's insecurities and she enjoyed putting them at ease. It took so little—a kind look, a gentle touch. Girls liked Grace too. She was voted both prom queen and the nicest girl in the senior class.

She was not comfortable sleeping with another woman's husband. She had not intended it to happen, but Joshua was so persuasive. He seemed to understand things that transcended life's customary rules. He understood that a beautiful woman with lots of friends can feel deeply alone; that she was constantly afraid of disappointing people so she always put others first; that physical beauty could be a terrible burden, since for most people it was so dazzling it was all they saw, obliterating the human being who was just as flawed and insecure as everybody else. Joshua understood what it felt like to be isolated by your gifts and that sometimes the only way to break out of that isolation is to break the rules; that you don't want to hurt others with your actions, but sometimes fate demands a surrender to illicit love. Grace believed this; she believed in Joshua; but now there were some questions.

She pressed the signal button, got off the gridlocked bus, and walked the last eight blocks to Frederic's building. Her time with Joshua was so limited, and she wasn't going to waste it stuck in traffic.

She hit the elevator button to the penthouse and checked herself in the security mirror. Grace liked clothes and looked good in her tight-fitting, black turtleneck cashmere sweater tucked into loose-cut black jeans. The black showed off her honey-blonde hair and creamy complexion. She wore no makeup except for lip gloss and a touch of mascara. She knew Joshua liked her natural elegance.

Joshua emerged from the bathroom clean and refreshed and grateful for the cold beer waiting on the kitchen table.

"To health!" toasted Frederic.

"To life!" answered Joshua. He'd never thought he could have so much: a beautiful baby, the school, a home, and a gorgeous girlfriend.

The elevator clanked and the doors opened.

Grace was used to being desired, but Joshua was the first man she had ever so thoroughly wanted in return. There was no part of his body she didn't crave. His smile turned her to mush and she struggled to remember her mission as she stepped out of the elevator into his open arms.

"There's my baby," said Joshua, enveloping her.

"Hi, Frederic," groaned Grace, embarrassed.

Frederic toasted them both. "I'll be in the den watching the game. You kids have fun." And he left the kitchen, closing the door behind him.

"Hi," said Joshua, refusing to let her go.

"Hi," said Grace, knowing she should struggle to get free. "Kind of smoky in here. Can we open some windows?"

Joshua looked into her eyes and said, "Sure. At least it's not cigars." He opened a window and the door to the servant's bedroom off the kitchen that Frederic had had Joshua turn into a guest bedroom with a private bath during the last renovation. When Joshua had washed up, he'd noticed the clean towels and candles. Frederic was a good friend. Joshua wondered how long it would take to get to the bedroom. He could tell Grace had a problem. She was probably worried about what they were doing to Judy. Grace cared about people. It was why he was so fond of her. And it would serve him right if she ended their affair. "So what's cooking?" he asked, waving smoke out the window.

"That's what you say in your classes," answered Grace, surprised.

Joshua shrugged and waited to hear the problem.

"I'm really glad to see you," said Grace. "I missed you."

"That can make our time together even sweeter," said Joshua, the twinkle coming back into his eyes. He stepped close, pushing his belly into hers.

"You know I believe in your abilities," said Grace.

"Sure," said Joshua, breathing in the scent of her hair.

"And I don't see energy or pick up so many of the things you do."

Joshua caressed her neck with his lips and wondered what any of this had to do with Judy.

"And I know that sometimes you know things about people, so you do things to help them that might appear—I don't know—a little strange."

Joshua nodded and waited.

"Do you know what I'm getting to?" asked Grace, praying he did and that he'd say something to make it all right—something funny so she'd laugh at how silly she was to worry about him and Harmony. Of course, she had once been his student also, but it was after they'd met at Frederic's. Also, Grace had far more experience than Harmony, and there was a mature feeling between her and Joshua. Grace wanted Joshua to say something that proved he wasn't a teacher badly abusing his authority and endangering a vulnerable student.

Joshua was thinking too hard to hear any of Grace's thoughts, so he shook his head and said, "I have no idea what you're getting at. Do you want to tell me?"

"It's whatever you were doing when you were standing over Harmony," blurted Grace. "What was that?"

"Oh," said Joshua, with a laugh. "That was nothing."

"But you were straddling her, Joshua. It looked sexual."

"So what else is new?" said Joshua, rocking her against his body.

"Joshua, I really need to understand this," said Grace, pushing out of his embrace. "If I didn't know better, from the way you were looking at her, I'd have thought you were having sex."

Joshua smiled. "Were you jealous?"

"No!" protested Grace. "I mean, yes, but that's not why I'm talking about this."

"It was nothing," said Joshua. "She's very repressed, and I was helping her connect with her sexuality."

Grace considered this. She badly wanted to believe it wasn't bullshit. After all, Joshua's unorthodox approach had helped her and so many others. She'd witnessed people with seemingly frozen defenses melting. There was the woman who hadn't smiled her whole life who now lit up a room; the lost souls found; the frightened finding courage. Yes, his methods seemed peculiar, but they worked, so shouldn't she trust that what looked like sex was in fact therapeutic work?

"Joshua, I work with Harmony."

"I know, and I thank you for bringing her to the school."

"What I'm trying to say is that you should be very careful. She may not understand that you are working with her as her teacher."

Chapter 23

MISSED CONTACT

Harmony moved piles of manuscripts from one side of her desk to the other, opened and closed her middle drawer, then opened it again and forgot why. Adrenaline burned through her heart. There was nowhere to run and nobody to confess to. How could she tell someone it was her fault Cora was back in the hospital due to the sudden, incomprehensibly fast growth of a tumor that had been in remission just a few days before? She didn't know why zapping it had made it grow, but she knew she'd done it, and she couldn't even tell Cora she was sorry without sounding insane.

She thought of calling Dr. Thompson and asking for an emergency session, but that didn't feel right. She needed to talk to somebody who knew more about this than she did, and that left only one choice.

Joshua rewound his voice mail and listened to the message again:

"Hi, Joshua, it's Harmony Rogers from your first year class. I think I may have done something really bad, and I need to talk to you. Call me as soon as you can."

"Shit," said Joshua. He had a whole morning of appointments and really didn't have time for a student's hysteria today . . . and particularly a student who wanted to confront him. What had he been thinking? Grace was right. But he couldn't dwell on that now. He'd find some rationale and call Harmony back at the noon break.

His first client was a new person—a sixty-five-year-old man whose presenting problem was prostate cancer, but Joshua took one look at his ballooning gut and collapsed chest, his sad, lifeless eyes and bulbous, alcoholic nose, and he knew this was not a cancer case. The man complained of back pains and asked if Joshua could do some manipulation to relieve his tension.

Joshua took a deep breath and exhaled slowly, letting go of all the assumptions, judgments, and expectations that had flooded his mind. It was crucial that he know nothing so he could just respond, comfort, be there for this soul. "I don't do manipulations like a chiropractor," he explained kindly. "My work is a little different. Why don't you tell me how your back feels, and we'll see what happens."

The man lay down on the massage table, closed his eyes, and began to tell Joshua about the tension—how it felt like a small animal being crushed, how there was no support, no help anywhere. As he spoke, Joshua watched the mud-brown energy weighing on the man's chest, the gray around his head, the black in his groin. Slowly, gently, Joshua began to sweep. He scooped and brushed as if cleaning years of dust off a priceless work of art, all the time not knowing—not knowing if the man would live or die, the reason for his illness, who was the healer and who was the healee. "Only know nothing," Rinpoche and his other Buddhist teachers had told him. Know only Love. Joshua swept and caressed and comforted, and finally stepped back in awe as a huge golden light like the sun at dawn slowly rose through the mud and gray and black. The man let out a raspy snore, and Joshua laughed. There were ten minutes before the next client, and he would let this great soul sleep. He wondered if his work was done . . . But he knew this was none of his business. He waited while the man snored.

Next was a woman who had been trying to conceive a baby for over three years. It was her fifth session with Joshua, and she was impatient. Joshua had been hoping for this. Instead of getting on the table and waiting for him to "fix" her, she paced and ranted about how she'd suspected all this energy crap was hooey, and she was sick and tired of people who promised miracles and took her money. Just when she was about to calm down, apologize, and get on the table like a good patient, Joshua asked if he reminded her of anyone else who made unrealistic promises and took what was hers. Then he sat back and watched as her face contorted with rage at his audacity to try "quack therapy" on her, because she'd been to plenty of shrinks like that last guy who not only said he could cure her infertility, but then had the gall to tell her it was her own fault that she couldn't get pregnant, and he said it all in that patronizing voice that was sickeningly reminiscent of her equally audacious father. And as she said this, Joshua watched the energetic hook that was imbedded in her uterus—a hook planted long before she could even remember, by her father—dissolve, leaving space for a baby. The woman stopped talking and breathed heavily. Then she wrote Joshua a check and announced that this was her last session. Joshua thanked her and wished her well with the sweet secret knowing that most likely she'd be pregnant this time next month.

Joshua had a special place in his heart for children, and he always scheduled them in the last slot so they could have extra time. Georgie was a six-year-old boy with autism who'd been coming every few weeks for the last couple of years. In the beginning, his mother would stay, sitting on the edge of her chair, praying for a miracle cure, but now she just dropped him off and enjoyed the opportunity to shop or get a haircut or have lunch with a friend. Georgie's father had left soon after his birth, so she didn't get much time for herself.

"Hi, Georgie!" said Joshua, in his most welcoming voice, and Georgie looked at the ceiling and opened and closed his fingers, which signaled that he heard.

"I'll see you in an hour," said Georgie's mother, kissing her son's unresponsive face. "Have a good time with your friend Joshua."

Joshua nodded and, as she did every time, she smiled brightly, swallowing tears, handed him a check, and left.

Joshua stood to the side of his open door and waited. By and by, Georgie wandered inside the office. He still didn't look at Joshua, but they both knew they were friends. Joshua closed the door softly because he knew Georgie didn't like loud noises. Then, clasping his hands behind his back, he strolled to the far side of the room, sat down on the floor in the pool of light reflected off the adjacent building, and leaned against the corner wall. And he waited.

Georgie dropped to the floor, clutched his knees, and began to rock, making a humming noise in the back of his mouth. His eyes flitted around the room, focusing on nothing.

"I love you, Georgie," murmured Joshua, and the humming got louder. Joshua admired Georgie's soft blonde curls and longed to hold the little boy the way he did Emily, but he knew it had to be Georgie's choice. And he waited . . . as he had been waiting for two years. He slumped back, opening his legs—the opposite of Georgie's clenched posture—and he waited.

Georgie's energy swirled in closed, compulsive loops around his upper body. There was no movement at all in the lower half. And he rocked and hummed and moaned.

Joshua imagined Georgie suddenly looking at him and succumbing to the exhaustion of six years. He could almost feel Georgie falling into his heart, letting Joshua hold and support him. How good it would feel to wrap his arms around that knotted little body as it relaxed.

Of all the chachkas on his shelves, his favorites were from Judy: the embroidered heart pillows, antique wind-up toys, and last Valentine's Day's small brass Tibetan singing bowl. On an impulse, Joshua reached for its little wood and cloth wand and gave the bowl an ever so gentle tap. *Ding*, went the bowl—a high, prolonged, sweet tone that wafted through the atmosphere.

Georgie abruptly stopped rocking and for one amazing moment, made eye contact with Joshua, who tried to remember to breathe. "Hi, Georgie," he whispered. But Georgie didn't answer. Joshua could feel the boy's confusion, but he decided to risk increasing it, and he dinged the bowl again—slightly louder. And again Georgie focused. "Would you like to do it?" asked Joshua, holding out the wand and bowl, and to his amazement, Georgie reached for them. "You have to come get them," said Joshua.

And for the first time in two years, the little boy spoke. "Mine," he said.

"That's right," encouraged Joshua, containing a heart burst. "It's yours. Just come and get it."

And the little boy climbed to his feet and, arms outstretched, walked to Joshua and plopped down between his legs, making his first voluntary physical contact with anyone besides his mother.

"Do you want to make it ding?" asked Joshua, trying to act like this was an everyday occurrence.

Georgie clasped the bowl in his fat hands and stared at it like it was a treasure. Then he spun around on his behind and fell against Joshua's chest.

"Would you like the wand?" asked Joshua, looking to the heavens as he carefully placed one arm around the little boy's torso. Georgie grabbed the wand out of Joshua's other hand and tried to bang the bowl. "Hold it at the end, sweetheart," said Joshua, arranging the boy's clumsy fingers around the wooden end. "That's right. Now tap it." Joshua guided Georgie's hand and together they made the bowl sing.

"Oooo," cooed Georgie, and he did it again himself. Then he craned his neck to look backwards up into Joshua's face.

"That was very good," said Joshua, kissing his forehead. And Georgie relaxed his knotted little body and sank into Joshua's heart.

Joshua would have held Georgie for the rest of his life if he could have, but Georgie's mother was prompt. At five minutes to twelve she knocked on the door.

"Come in," called Joshua as softly as he could.

He'd hoped Georgie's mother would be happy, but he understood when she burst into tears. "He never let me do that," she cried.

Joshua explained how Georgie lived in a private place. He was like a boy in a tree house, a cat up a pole. And the only way to make contact was to be invited to by him. Georgie's mother protested that she never forced, and Joshua understood her frustration. "He's like a scared wild animal," he explained. "It wasn't me. It was the sound that made him feel safe." And he gave her the singing bowl to take home and kissed her on the forehead. And Georgie's mother cried and thanked him, and by the time she left, it was five minutes before his first afternoon client, and he had completely forgotten about Harmony Rogers's emergency.

Chapter 24

RUTH

Cora was ecstatic. She had been discharged from the hospital a day after being admitted when, just before surgery, her tumor had shrunk as incomprehensibly quickly as it had grown. The doctors were mystified, but everybody was happy.

Harmony was furious. She had never felt entitled to anything in her life, but she felt entitled to a phone call from Joshua responding to her distress. She had tried to leave a second and third message, but had been unable to speak at the sound of the damned beep. Plus which, *she* knew he had received her first message and was ignoring her because he was attracted to her but couldn't handle it.

She was glad Cora had recovered, but this did nothing to mitigate her rage at Joshua. By the time she got to class three weeks after leaving the voice mail, she was afraid to look at him lest her eye energy set him on fire. She was too angry to be upset that the morning session was taught by a student assistant, or that there was a new person in class despite the fact that they were four months into the program. She (the new student) was joining the class late due to extenuating circumstances, said the student teacher, who didn't feel it necessary to share what those circumstances might be.

Harmony calculated what the refund would be when she quit after this weekend, and she combed her memory for how she knew the new person—a fifty-some-year-old woman with bad skin and pouches under her eyes.

When Joshua looked in just before the lunch break, Harmony felt her whole body sizzle with anger. He told the class they were to begin a homework assignment—recording their healing experiences. Hank sarcastically asked if they would be graded, and Joshua laughed and said, no, but added that sharing reinforces growth. Then he asked how everybody was doing. Harmony let loose a puff of anger, and before he could catch himself, Joshua said, "Harmony?"

"I need to talk to you," said Harmony, not caring if her laser-beam eyes did burn him. She felt Joshua suddenly remember her phone message and blush. Her thoughts spasmed. He forgot? How dare he forget?!

"Excuse me," erupted the new woman, and Harmony wished her dead. "Are you Joshua Gardner? I'm Ruth Gabriel. I left you a message, and you said I could join the class—"

Ruth Gabriel, of course—the woman from crazy Luanne's class who'd lost her son. Damn Joshua! He called a complete stranger back, but not her.

"Yes, of course," answered Joshua, addressing Ruth. "Welcome."

"I came because I thought you'd be teaching the class. I wasn't expecting . . . 'this,'" she said, attempting to make her disgust sound polite and gesturing generally in the direction of the student teachers.

Go, girl, thought Harmony, and she sat back to watch the confrontation.

Joshua looked hard at Ruth.

Shit, thought Harmony, he's going to get around it.

"What is it you expected to get here that you're not getting?" asked Joshua. His tone was gentle like a doting daddy.

"I— It's just . . ." She was fighting tears.

"Do you mind if I share with the class the message you left on the phone?" asked Joshua. His words caressed Ruth, who nodded her head like a child. "Ruth's son disappeared five years ago on his way to school, and she hoped she could learn enough psychic perception to either find him, or if he has passed on, to communicate with him."

Ruth collapsed and sobbed into her hands the way she'd done at Luanne's, but Joshua didn't tell her she had to accept God's will. Instead, he walked over to her, stood behind her chair, and emitted a glow from his heart that enveloped Ruth in a cocoon of light. The students who could see energy gasped, and those who couldn't wished they could, sensing that something miraculous was happening.

"You need to rest," said Joshua softly. And Ruth cried and cried.

When it was over, Ruth hugged Joshua and thanked him. You couldn't say exactly what had happened, and Joshua didn't try to.

Like everyone else, Harmony loved Joshua. How could you not? And she hated him for using his love so manipulatively. It was real, but it was cunning. You couldn't say exactly how, and Harmony didn't try to. She just "knew." She knew because she and Joshua were the same animal.

At the lunch break, she asked him why he hadn't called her back, and when he had a coughing fit in response, she pretended to be concerned and offered to get him tea. Then she asked again. And when he said he simply hadn't had time, she just looked at him. She waited while students interrupted with questions for Joshua, and she pretended not to know that he gave them such sudden, undivided attention because he was avoiding her. After he finished answering everyone else's questions, he apologetically told her he couldn't talk just now because he had a lunch meeting, and Harmony asked when he would be able to talk. He hemmed and hawed about how busy he was, and she said she really needed to talk to him and would wait by his office after the afternoon session. And she sensed that this was about more than Cora's tumor, but exactly what that "more" was eluded her.

Afternoon class was scheduled from one to six, but at 6:15, Joshua told everyone to move the chairs to the wall, and he pulled out conga drums. Then one of the assistants hooked up a microphone and some sang while others drummed. It sounded like an African jungle, and Harmony, who was the blackest one in the school except for Ruth, who'd left at the lunch break, felt embarrassed at her lack of soul as everyone around her exploded into gyrations, pelvises thrusting and torsos undulating and moves that harkened to an African fertility dance. Harmony, who was a very good dancer with Kathy Smith in the privacy of her living room, flashed to the twenty-five–foot woman of her vision with Dr. Thompson, but there was no way she was going to dance like that among people.

"Having a good time?" It was Joshua standing behind her. "Come on, dance with me." He moved his feet and wiggled suggestively.

Harmony blushed. "I'm not very big on public body motion."

Joshua smiled and took little swaying steps, inviting her to join him. Reluctantly, Harmony began. First, just shifting from side to side, then a kind of gentle to and fro of her hips, then her arms went up and out as if to catch something. The drums were drumming, and she felt the pounding shoot up between her legs. Her face filled with blood, her body throbbed and pulsated, and her eyes rolled back, blind with excitement.

Drums drummed, and Joshua, who had thought he would invite Harmony to dance to communicate that he valued her and that a public exchange of sensual energy was nothing to be upset about, but rather was highly therapeutic—so she would let the missed phone call along with the whole upset go—watched with a dropped jaw, suddenly realizing who this was and why he kept fantasizing her nursing breasts.

Grace, standing in a corner with a couple of the assistants, quietly excused herself and went home.

Chapter 25

FINDING TRIBE

At the end of the dance, Harmony asked Joshua about the results of her zapping Cora's tumor. He had a strange expression on his face, but he gave a comprehensive answer:

Cancer cells are anarchists, he explained. They've forgotten that they're part of a system, so instead of allowing energy to nurture them and flow on, they hoard it and reproduce. So zapping cancer actually fuels its growth. The way to deal with a tumor is to envelope it with light; make it feel welcome; then invite it to merge, dissipating its mass.

He said all this in such a strange monotone that Harmony forgot to tell him she was quitting the school, and she didn't remember that she forgot until she was getting into bed a few hours later.

"Damn," she said, remembering the refund. A refund and no tuition meant that she might be able to quit her damned job. Hell, she'd quit therapy. Maybe she'd quit everything.

Then she remembered the feeling of the drums when she danced and thought, what the hey, maybe she'd give it another month. And she *had* to get back to damned Kathy Smith.

Bedtime was when Harmony missed Delilah most. It was a deep, physical longing for Delilah's soft body nestled against her right side. Harmony still hadn't taken down the jerry-rigged ramp to the bed that Delilah had used since she'd lost the spring in her hind legs. Every night it was the same thing— Harmony would step up the ramp feeling that pain in the middle of her chest like something was broken and bleeding. It scared her, so sometimes she got up and ate. Or watched TV. Sometimes she played. For years she'd found children's miniature toy animals dropped in playgrounds and on footpaths in Central Park. She had glow-in-the-dark frogs and a crocodile with a movable mouth and several kinds of dinosaurs, fish, monkeys, birds, and snakes.

They were arranged on stones in a ceramic bowl water garden on top of her bureau. When she couldn't sleep, she would sometimes rearrange them so the crocodile was eating one of the frogs, or a fish was edging its way over the rim of the bowl, or the tiniest monkey was being lifted on high by several snakes. She'd made the bowl in a pottery class, then turned it into a water garden by placing a small fish tank pump in the center, layering stones around it so the water spouted and trickled making a sound like a running stream. She liked the animals pointing in different directions, and recently she'd added a small troll. She'd half-submerged him so his raised arms seemed to protest the entire situation. Sometimes playing with her toy figures made her forget to miss Delilah for a while. Sometimes she didn't play but just lay awake all night.

Tonight, she was too tired—too tired to play, too tired to feel afraid of the feeling in her chest, too tired to run away from it. She lay in her bed in the pitch black room letting the feeling spread. It was like being split apart from the inside out by a very sharp carving knife. It was as if her whole body were menstruating—bleeding and throbbing with pain. It was intolerable, except she was too exhausted to be intolerant.

And suddenly, it hit her how lucky she was to have this nice dark room where there was enough heat, her rent was stabilized, and there was enough night for her to lie in her soft bed listening to the trickle of her water garden, consumed with pain. She didn't have to get up and do anything. She could just lie here. There was a soft pressure—a presence—against her right side. A softness that felt like love. It pushed against her ribs, and she remembered how it was when Delilah lay down to sleep. She remembered that moment when Delilah's whole body would melt into her side and she'd drift off to sleep. She remembered the night that Delilah had left her body. Harmony felt her leave. She saw the last breath, and no matter how hard she loved, she could not go with her. When she tried, she felt the force—a strong masculine force—it said, "No" and it pushed her back into her body. The pain of the memory split her heart right down the center, and her whole chest turned into a pulsing pool of blood. She could hear it whooshing so loud it filled the room. She knew she was not asleep and this was not a dream. She could see nothing; the room was black. She put a hand on her chest. It wasn't wet or sticky, but it was hot. Very, very hot. She thought about turning on a light, but a voice—a strong, masculine voice—said, "No." The whooshing turned into a roar in her ears, and then she heard the drums. Her uterus spasmed and blood shot out between her legs. She tried to get up to make a run for the bathroom, but the voice said, "No," and the force pressed her down into the mattress.

Her breasts hurt from a pressure under her nipples, and she was afraid they were going to spit blood too. If only she could turn on a light, but her arms were pinned. The drums beat louder—congas like at the school dance—syncopated, complicated, intricate patterns. Her breasts were in agony, and she writhed. Her uterus contracted, and she was sure she would have to buy a new mattress in the morning. She ran her parched tongue over her lips and they felt swollen.

When she felt upset, Harmony liked to think about Hillary Rodham Clinton. She really admired Hillary and was so glad she'd won the race for the Senate. Harmony thought Hillary's dignity and ability to stay married to Bill and not commit homicide would make her an excellent representative. No matter how much Hillary felt, she always contained it and stayed human. Lying in bed, splitting apart, Harmony wished to be like a lone, strong Hillary Rodham Clinton. "No," said the voice, "it's take a village," and Harmony almost fell off the bed.

As Harmony laughed, she saw a vision of Hillary's smiling face. Then the face split apart, and out came three black women, and they danced in a circle around the bed.

All her life, Harmony had feared going insane. Now it was happening and she didn't fight it.

"It's time to dance, pretty girl," said the largest woman.

"No!" roared Harmony.

"She won't dance; don't ask her," sang another woman in a high soprano like she was in a Broadway musical.

Then the third woman, who had blue-black skin and hands the size of baseball mitts, reached into Harmony's chest and cradled her heart.

"No!" screamed Harmony, pulling away. But it was useless. The three black women reached for Harmony's heart with hands that radiated light, and they enveloped it, inviting it to merge into their light. And that was the last thing Harmony remembered.

The next day was Monday, a work day. Harmony woke pre-dawn and was surprised that she didn't have her period and her sheets were clean. She did a whole hour of Kathy Smith, changing the jumps into no-impact aerobic bends and slides in order not to wake her downstairs neighbors, then she washed, dressed, and left a voicemail for Joseph that she was sick. At 6:30 a.m., she boarded a pre-rush hour bus that flew uptown, and she got off at 72nd Street and headed for Central Park.

It was a frigid February day—not the best weather for a stroll—but she felt drawn to the trees. She blew on her frozen fingers and headed west along the path she'd walked so many times with Delilah. At the Boathouse, she turned north up the hill to the Ramble, a wooded area shared by dog walkers, bird watchers, and gay men having sex in the bushes.

It had been a virtually snowless winter, but there were icicles sparkling on the trees and the brown ground was frozen so solid it didn't even crack under Harmony's L.L. Bean hiking boots as she ignored the signs to stay on the paths and cut through the woods to the Ramblehut. The Ramblehut was a shelter made of rough-hewn tree limbs where homeless people sometimes camped. She prayed it would be empty and odorless. She wanted to sit by herself on the worn slab benches with her boots in the dirt.

Yes! It was empty. And even though it stank from misuse, she sat down, took off her gloves, and stuck her frozen fingers in her mouth. And that's when she remembered that today was her forty-third birthday.

This is what life had come to: she was a middle-aged orphan with no dog and a job she hated, sitting alone in a hut in the woods in New York City at seven o'clock in the morning inhaling urine. And she began to cry.

"So are you Black or White?" said a voice behind her.

Only a Black person would be so direct. "Black," answered Harmony without turning or flinching so maybe the person would go away. Suddenly she was flattened by a hurtling ball of Golden Retriever pinning her against the bench, hysterically licking her face.

"Holy shit!" yelled Harmony.

"Fido, get down. I'm sorry," said the dog's person, grabbing for his collar. "I didn't mean to scare you."

"Hi," said Harmony, seeing who it was.

"I was at the healing school yesterday. Ruth Gabriel. And you are?"

"Harmony Rogers," said Harmony, amazed.

"Small world."

"Yeah, I guess. Don't worry about Fido. I like dogs."

Ruth sat down with a squishing sound. She took up half the bench. Harmony hadn't noticed how bottom-heavy she was.

"Kind of cold to be hanging out if you don't have no dog," said Ruth, blowing hot air on her hands and pulling off her ski hat.

"I had a dog," said Harmony.

"Oh," said Ruth. "Sorry."

Harmony wondered if Ruth had gotten her dog after her son's disappearance or if she'd always been a dog person.

"Fido's alls I've got left of my son," said Ruth. "The two of them was like brothers."

"I'm sorry," said Harmony, wondering if she'd missed something and Ruth was a thought-talker.

"Don't see many Black folk at these healing type places," said Ruth, coaxing Fido into a down position and resting a foot on his back.

Harmony considered lying, but she was too tired. "To tell you the truth, I don't know what I am. I was adopted."

"Hmm," said Ruth.

"I'm sorry about your son," said Harmony, and she really meant it.

"Thanks," said Ruth.

"Why'd you leave yesterday?" asked Harmony. "You disappeared after lunch."

Ruth shifted uncomfortably. "Something about that guy. I don't know."

"Joshua?"

"Yeah, him."

Both women were silent for a minute, then Harmony finally said it: "He's very sexy."

"A little too sexy, if you ask me," said Ruth, raising an eyebrow.

Harmony laughed. "So you didn't find what he did helpful?"

"Oh no, it wasn't that. That was very nice."

"So?" Harmony knew the answer, but she wanted to hear Ruth say it.

"The man's a dog. I'll bet he's married."

"So I've heard," said Harmony.

"That's the worst kind," said Ruth, pursing her lips with disgust. "But who am I to judge? To each his own, I always say. And if I thought he could find my son, I'd pay the damn tuition and let those white people teach me. What the hell was that anyhow? Ain't a school supposed to have real teachers?! That was almost as bad as the Reiki lady."

Harmony laughed so hard she thought she was going to be sick. "I didn't think you remembered."

"Oh, I remembered all right. Just didn't think it was worth my mentioning. You thought I was gullible, didn't you?"

Harmony blushed.

"I know when somebody's taking my inventory. All's I want to know is what happened to my son. I ain't dumb."

"I'm sorry," said Harmony.

"S'okay," said Ruth.

Fido fell asleep and both women breathed.

"Nothing like the smell of fresh piss on a clear winter morning," said Ruth.

"Do you want to walk?" asked Harmony stretching her legs. "I used to come here every weekend with Delilah."

"That your dog?" asked Ruth, waking Fido and snapping on his leash.

Harmony nodded. "I'm playing hooky today."

"How about we go over to the rock pool behind the Azalea Pond? It's still too early for the park Gestapo, and Fido likes to swim."

The Azalea Pond was a prime bird-watching location where ardent birders had wired feeders to the stratospheric treetops. They hung like strange aluminum mobiles from the bare winter branches, reflecting in the pond. There were no birders here this morning and not much action among the birds who were almost invisible perched in the upper branches.

The rock pool was a small receptacle for water running south from the Reservoir on its way down to the big lake. Even though it was 28 degrees, Fido belly-flopped into the rock pool and paddled down to the deep end where a blasé New York City duck was napping. The duck ignored Fido until he was within snapping distance, then sounded one disdainful quack and flew off. Fido barked, swimming victory circles around the deep end, then bounded up the rocks and out of the pool. He shook joyfully, showering Ruth and Harmony with filthy, icy water.

"So you know something about this E.S.P. stuff?" asked Ruth, wiping her face.

"Maybe a little," said Harmony, taken aback. "I'm interested in energy. That's about it."

"Energy. You mean like auras and all?"

"Sure," said Harmony. "I just think it's interesting. But I don't know very much."

Ruth pursed her lips. "You ever hear of the African Bushmen?"

Harmony felt uneasy. She hadn't picked up any thoughts and had no idea where this was going. "Bushmen? You mean those little guys?"

"I don't know how big they are. All's I know is they travel around the Kalahari Desert and they communicate with energy. I read a book about it. You ever heard of that?"

Harmony didn't know if she was more scared or excited. "What did the book say?"

"It said the Bushmen communicate through energy lines coming out of their belly buttons, and the lines connect to everything and everybody. It's like phone lines, only wireless. So say for instance some of them go hunting and they kill a bear—"

"I don't think they have bears in the Kalahari."

"You know, you're a pain in the butt," snapped Ruth. "Shut your mouth and let me finish."

Harmony liked this woman.

"Anyway, like I was saying—suppose one of them kills some animal to eat. All they do is they radio back through the energy lines, and when they get back to their camp where all the lady Bushmen are waiting, the fires are set to cook."

"You read this in a book?"

"Yep," said Ruth. "Don't remember the name of it, but it was there in writing. So I figure if we're all connected to everything, if I could just find the right person to follow the right line, I could find Billy."

There was a strange lull in the wind, then a sudden rush as sleeping birds woke and took off en masse.

"I always wonder what makes them do that," said Harmony, looking up.

"Probably 'sense' something. . . . You ever sense things?"

"Sure," said Harmony, wondering what time it was and suddenly remembering she hadn't eaten breakfast. "You know, it's my birthday? You want to go to the Boathouse for hot chocolate? My treat."

"Sure," said Ruth. "But we got to set outside in the cold. They don't let dogs in."

The Boathouse outdoor café was deserted except for crazy Annie, a benign schizophrenic who lived in the park with five dogs. She was well known by dog walkers and tolerated by park rangers. Harmony and Ruth spotted her sitting in the corner having a conversation on a twig phone. They looked at each other, shrugged, and Harmony headed for hot chocolate.

"Angels!" shrieked Annie, waving like a four-year-old. "My angels!"

"Hi, Annie," called Harmony. "How're you doing?"

Annie's face suddenly dropped. "They say your dog died," she said sadly. "I'm sorry." Then she broke the twig in many pieces and threw it on the ground. "Damn cell phones. Nothing but bad news."

Ruth shivered and planted herself on an icy metal chair.

Annie dug through her shopping bags for a new phone and instead pulled out two old baseball mitts which she happily put on either hand. She put one hand to her ear and the other on her heart, and listened.

"It's too cold for this," said Ruth to nobody.

A few minutes later, Harmony returned with three steaming cups of hot chocolate. She handed one to Ruth and put another down beside Annie.

"Happy birthday," said Annie. "They say you're too judgmental. And you need to dance."

Harmony gulped hot chocolate and burned her mouth. "Thanks," she said, then returned to Ruth who was sipping carefully and pushing Fido away from her cup.

"Too hot?" asked Harmony.

"It'll keep my hands warm," said Ruth.

"Also, they say you should have real sex!" shrieked Annie, breaking into gales of laughter, and all five dogs jumped to their feet and barked. "Sex! Sex! Sex!" screamed Annie. The dogs looked at her, then lay back down.

Harmony stared hard at Ruth. "Would you think I was crazy if I said I had sex with Joshua through those energy lines?"

Ruth stopped mid-sip, and slowly her mouth spread into a Cheshire cat grin. "Well, that's a new way to have a good time with a dog like that."

"It's not exactly an affair, so you can't say I'm sleeping with another woman's husband. I think it's kind of creative," said Harmony. And both women slapped their thighs and laughed. Alarmed, Fido started barking. Then Annie's dogs erupted, and Annie screamed, "Sex!" Then everybody shut up.

"So where do you work?" asked Harmony after a minute. "How do you manage to be in the park on a weekday?"

"I'm a freelance bookkeeper," said Ruth, smiling over her paper cup. "I'm very good at tallying things up, so my clients let me set my own schedule."

"That's the life," said Harmony, thinking about her Teflon tomb cubicle.

"How about yourself?" asked Ruth.

"I tidy."

"Come again."

"I work at a magazine. They call me managing editor, but really, I just tidy. It's very boring. I want to quit."

"What do you want to do instead?"

Harmony shrugged. "I wish I knew. Do you think there's a career for energy sex prostitutes?"

Ruth laughed and drained the last of her hot chocolate.

"You know, if I knew any way to find your son, I would," said Harmony.

"Would you at least try?" pleaded Ruth. She yanked a locket out from under her coat and struggled to open it with frozen fingers. "This is Billy."

Harmony stared at the beautiful six-year-old boy.

"Memorize that face," commanded Ruth. Then she closed the locket and tucked it back under her coat.

Harmony thought for a while. "I don't even know how I do what I do do," she said helplessly.

"Do-do?" said Ruth.

"Shit!" screamed Annie.

"Maybe we should just try," said Harmony.

"Okay," said Ruth, and the two women closed their eyes.

"No!" shrieked Annie, bursting into tears. "Angels on fire. One-two-three-jump! Oh no!"

And in any place other than New York City, people might have stopped and stared. But neither dog walkers going up the hill to the Ramble for their morning romps, nor restaurant delivery men bringing supplies to the Boathouse, nor half-asleep tourists buying coffees even paused at the sight of the three women—one large black one, one of indeterminate race, and one with blue-black skin whose baseball-mitted hands cradled her heart. They sat with eyes closed, weeping while six dogs slept, their slow breaths hanging in white clouds in the freezing morning air.

Chapter 26

JOSHUA'S DREAM

Four years ago when Joshua was forty-three, he had a dream that he'd never forgotten:

It was soon after his marriage to Judy, but in the dream, Emily was already born. (He often dreamed people before they physically appeared in his life.) He was in a backyard that had an old-fashioned well. His mother was sitting in a lawn chair drinking tea, and Judy was nursing the baby. Suddenly, the sky darkened with angry looking gray clouds. His mother screamed, "Save the baby! Save the baby!" and in response, Judy threw Emily down the well.

"No!" screamed Joshua, diving in after her. He fell and fell, down and down this bottomless, black hole, but no matter how fast he fell, he never caught up to the baby who was screaming in terror. Joshua tried to call to her, but no sound would come out. He lost all sense of direction and was just falling in the black. Gradually he could no longer hear the baby, and realizing she was gone, he cried—but still without sound. And just when he thought this would be his life—falling forever—he saw light. At the bottom of the hole was a woman—a light-skinned Black woman with radiant eyes. She was wearing bright red shoes, standing with arms spread to catch the baby. And *thwunk*! The baby landed in her arms. Crying with joy, Joshua floated gently down after the baby.

"Hello," said the woman. "I'll see you later." She handed him the baby, and he woke up.

The woman was Black, but she looked vaguely like Hillary Clinton, Joshua realized as he contemplated the dream now, four years later, the night after dancing with Harmony Rogers.

Joshua had always had a soft spot for Bill Clinton. He thought Bill got a really raw deal after the Monica Lewinsky affair. The man was lonely. And maybe it was love. Who's to judge? Maybe the affair was karma or destiny or whatever you want to call it—a bargain sealed between two people long before they incarnated, to help each other in some mysterious way.

Harmony Rogers was shorter than Hillary Clinton. Darker. And stranger. Lord, she was driving him crazy. What if that dream was a reminder of a long-forgotten agreement? What if she was some kind of earth mother black goddess African something-or-other? Who's to say? And what if he *did* want her? It wasn't a crime; he was only human. The main thing was he would not act like Bill Clinton. *He* could control his impulses. He would do the right thing. Harmony had such marvelous potential, but she'd spent her life in isolation. He was her healer. He would help her, and she in turn might help others. The outcome was none of his business.

He rolled over and watched Judy sleep. She was a beautiful woman. His priorities were in order.

Chapter 27

JOSEPH

Almost a month had passed since Harmony's last class. March workshops were next weekend, and she'd procrastinated to the last minute asking for the following Monday off. By now, she realized it took days to recover from these weekends, so perhaps it was better to arrange vacation ahead of time instead of feigning illness. Joseph Timiani was still mellow since returning from the Bahamas, so maybe this was good timing.

Harmony made sure all queries were answered, all manuscripts trafficked to the appropriate editors, all invoices paid, new deadlines posted. Then she went to the ladies' room to be quiet and fortify herself for the conversation with Joseph. Even if he was in a good mood, he could get testy at intrusions. Sometimes it was fine, but other times it could seem fine, and you'd say something really straight-forward like, "Do you want me to reject that submission?" and he'd hear it all twisted and snap, "I will *not* be forced into decisions to accommodate *your* schedule! It's an intuitive process that I do in my *own* time. You work for *me*!" It was such a response that made Harmony decide to speak only when spoken to. It wasn't that she was afraid of Joseph. She just hated feeling his energetic acid in her face.

She stared in the ladies' room mirror and concentrated on finding the energetic line to Ruth. She really liked Ruth. They hadn't found her son, but at least they'd found each other. She knew Ruth wouldn't feel her connecting, but she still felt better the instant she did it. She breathed in Ruth's bulk and prepared to ask for Monday off.

Joseph surveyed his orderly desktop and made a brisk, satisfied nodding motion with his head. Then, remembering his vow to hold his head still, he stretched upward as if a string were pulling the top of his skull, and he readjusted in his chair. His least favorite part of aging was his turkey neck, and his hair stylist had recommended a posture therapist who said if he stopped excess motion and stretched, he could begin to firm the baggy skin. Walter, his new lover, pretended not to care, but Joseph was painfully aware of their twenty-year age difference, and he simply could not bear having his heart broken again. He was contemplating a face lift, hair plugs, and Botox injections when Harmony Rogers knocked on his open office door nearly giving him a coronary.

"Excuse me, Joseph, is this a bad time?"

"No," gasped Joseph, suddenly feeling very strange.

"Well, I wondered if it would be all right if, instead of taking the rest of my vacation time in blocks, I took it in many single days—Mondays, to be specific—starting a week from this coming Monday. I know this is last minute, but I've made a list which I've checked against our production schedule, and I don't see any conflicts." Joseph stared at her. "Here's the list." Joseph said nothing, but stared, glassy-eyed. "Okay, then," said Harmony, quickly placing the list on his desk and retreating. "Let me know. I didn't mean to bother you." And she left.

Since she'd done all her work in the first hour, Harmony decided to spend the rest of the day writing her homework assignment about her most healing experiences. She liked writing her experiences, so this might be fun. She thought for a long time, and then typed:

> I know that to be a good person, you're supposed to be good, to
> help, to do no harm, to be part of a family, to not think other peo-
> ple are stupid or boring, to not feel superior, selfish, or intolerant.

> I am not a good person. I don't like most of the people in my
> class. Well, that's not true. I'm indifferent. The only reason I
> enrolled in this school was to have somebody to talk to in my
> own language—thoughts or energy. Also, I'm very horny due to
> a peculiar energy missile that goes up between my legs, and the
> energy sex has been nice. A relief actually.

> I know that energy etiquette requires not speaking of subtle
> things out loud. For instance, our energy sex or the dream meet-

ings or that first thought-exchange on the bus. But I do want to say on paper that I find these to be my most healing experiences.

Also, to be completely truthful, I do enjoy some people in my class. I enjoyed doing healing on Roxana, and I met that woman Ruth Gabriel outside of school and enjoy spending time with her. Grace is not technically in my class, but I like her also.

Perhaps this is not what you meant when you asked us to record our healing experiences. But it's the truth. And what's the point if I don't tell the truth?

Harmony started to hit the print button, but had a second thought:

In the interest of truth, there is one more thing. I'm saying this because I really admire and respect you.

I think the school would do better if you'd hired professional teachers instead of volunteer students to teach classes. Having student teachers makes you the only authority.

You have said that bringing our secret intentions into awareness makes us grow. If there is nobody in the school who can challenge you about your secret intentions, how will you ever grow? How will you get out of your cage?

I liked falling off the table. I liked catching people also. I think I'm a fairly good catcher. When are you going to fall?

She hit the print key, then deleted the document. She knew it sounded primitive and she should probably re-work it. She knew it didn't read like any homework she'd ever imagined. But on an impulse, she put the paper in a *Your Garden* envelope addressed to Joshua, and by the time she changed her mind, the four o'clock mail collector had already picked it up.

Cora was out today, and Harmony hadn't heard boo from Joseph. She didn't want to bother him again, but she decided to stroll by his office and see if he was still here. If he wasn't, maybe she'd sneak out early.

"Oh jeez!" she exclaimed, running into his office. "Oh jeez, Joseph; oh jeez!"

It took the paramedics twenty-five minutes to get their gurney up the freight elevator, then another ten to maneuver it into Joseph's office. "Looks like a stroke," said the tall one.

Joseph was sitting in the same strange stretched-neck position he was in when Harmony had seen him this morning, and he stared unblinking through glassy, blue eyes.

Harmony had a dilemma: to remain quiet or to relay his silent screaming. "He says he's allergic to Latex," she finally blurted.

The paramedics gave each other a look. "I didn't hear nothin'," said the short one.

"I mean he once told me that. In the past. In conversation," said Harmony.

"Oh, hell," said the short paramedic, and the two ripped off their rubber gloves. "Do you know if he got any transmittable diseases? AIDS, Hepatitis—"

"No!" thought-screamed Joseph.

"No!" barked Harmony. "He has no diseases."

"You seem to know a lot about your boss," said the tall paramedic suspiciously.

"Yes, we're close personal friends," said Harmony, wondering how she'd recover from this if Joseph didn't die.

And it was with that exact thought, in that exact moment, that she suddenly knew the big truth was that there is no such thing as death. The knowing lasted only a second—a sudden but timeless blink when she and Joseph and the paramedics and the room faded so that what normally appeared real looked ghostly, fuzzy—like a kind of light reflection from something too big to describe. And there was a smell. Gardenias? And in that timeless perfumed blink, Harmony realized that life was just a funny play of reflections, and no doubt, with no death, she would see Joseph forever and ever, so she was eternally screwed. "Oh crap," she whispered.

"I said, do you know his next of kin?" bellowed the tall paramedic for the third time as he and his partner tried to jockey the gurney through Joseph's narrow door.

"Call Walter Fortis in accounting!" thought-yelled Joseph. "For God's sake, are you deaf?!"

"Okay!" yelled Harmony.

"What?" said the tall paramedic, giving his partner another look of incredulity.

"Yes. I mean no. He has a friend in accounting. I'll call and ask him to meet you at the hospital," said Harmony.

"Don't tell them we're gay!" thought-yelled Joseph.

"They're gay!" blurted Harmony. "Both him and his friend."

"Whatever," said the short paramedic, and they disappeared down the hall.

Chapter 28

JUDGMENT CALL

It had been a week since Joseph had been carted away. Friday afternoon, Harmony had jotted copious notes for Cora, phoned everybody who needed to be alerted and then some, and announced she would be taking Monday off but said that everything was taken care of and she would be back Tuesday. As a backup to her emails, she'd left multiple hard copies of alphabetized story lists with complete author contact information for all the editors and production people, tidied her desk, and left. Friday night, and again Saturday morning, she'd studied the names on the class contact sheet before leaving her apartment, so now, as she looked around the circle at the faces, she knew who everyone was. Crystal, the woman who'd had polio, looked a little less hateful; Hank was yawning; and Roxana looked healthy. They exchanged smiles as Joshua entered and took his seat in between the assistant teachers, Martha and Roger. Harmony was pleased that she remembered names she had never spoken. She felt tense but happy as she waited for Joshua's smile and his "What's cooking?" He was wearing new pants that showed off his butt. He had the most beautiful—

"Harmony!" said Joshua.

It felt like a stab to her heart. "What?"

"You like my butt?"

Harmony blushed magenta. "Why, yes."

A confused discomfort shot around the circle.

"So what's cooking?" said Joshua, and several people coughed. "So what? She likes my butt. I'm flattered. So what's going on? What's happened since last month? I see Roxana's back. You look good."

Roxana blushed and said, thank you, she was feeling well.

Mortified, Harmony slouched in her chair and watched as Joshua smiled, and one by one people relaxed and spoke about their problems or questions or insights, as if nothing strange had happened and nobody had said the word "butt."

Sherry was complaining about her inability to lose weight and tearfully confessing that her husband wouldn't touch her anymore and she'd started taking amphetamines, when Joshua noticed out of the corner of his eye that Harmony's aura had virtually shut off. She'd looked like the sun when he'd walked in. Why had he made that butt comment? He'd just had to stick her for that nasty letter about his needing to be the only authority. The arrogance! But still, it was his job to transcend his reactions and help her out of her deluded judgments. He must make this right.

"Harmony!" he said, interrupting Sherry, who was so surprised she stopped crying mid-sob.

"What?" said Harmony, sitting upright.

"Are you with this?"

"With what?" asked Harmony, avoiding his eyes and dreading another surprise stab.

Joshua felt as if he'd slapped his baby. Somehow he'd fix this. "What do you think about Sherry's problem?"

"I, I don't know," stammered Harmony. She was not going to get trapped into saying something bad about somebody again. "I hope she stops hurting so much." Joshua looked at Harmony with soft eyes, and she felt her "watch out" alarm go off.

"What do you think about Sherry's husband not wanting to touch her?"

Harmony panicked. What did she know of husbands and wives? She hadn't had physical sex in over five years, and before that it was just a few one-night stands. She was *not* going to talk about somebody else's sex life. "I, I don't know," she answered. "I'm not married."

"You could still have an opinion," said Joshua patiently.

The class was beginning to shift and shuffle their feet. Sherry was frowning.

"Maybe Sherry has more to say about it," said Harmony hopefully.

"So you don't have any opinions on sexual relationships?"

"Why are you doing this?" thought-talked Harmony, but Joshua persisted.

"Sexuality is a normal part of life. There's no reason to be embarrassed about these things."

Harmony stared daggers at him.

"Or maybe it's a normal part of life for everybody but Harmony."

"Maybe I prefer to keep those things to myself," she said in a voice that sent shivers up everyone but Joshua's back.

Joshua was enjoying this. "Or maybe you don't have *real* relationships with members of the opposite sex, so you have nothing to talk about."

There are a few times in your life when you have the clarity to realize that you are poised at an emotional crossroads. Maybe it was the shock of Joshua's statement that threw Harmony into such a moment. She paused. And instead of shattering into a million pieces or blowing a gasket and yelling "You miserable sonofabitch bastard, what the hell do you think you are doing?" she just looked at Joshua and saw the big picture: He didn't have a clue what he was doing. And seeing this dissolved all bad feelings.

"Maybe I just haven't met the right man yet," said Harmony softly and watched as Joshua tried to hide his confusion. "Maybe I'd rather live with no sex than act on a string of infatuations, always feeling empty afterwards, because it wasn't really love after all. How could it be when the person couldn't even hear me?"

Joshua stared at her. He was torn between wanting to hurt her and wanting to jump on top of her. But instead, he turned to the rest of the class who were looking at each other in confusion and said, "So what's cooking?"

Harmony's moment of clarity passed, and she spent the rest of the day alternately embarrassed and furious that Joshua had publicly exposed her shameful lack of sexual experience. She was torn between wanting to hurt him and wanting to jump on top of him and show him exactly how passionate she felt and how she could make love with every cell of his and her own body.

Joshua pretended not to notice. He concentrated his energy on his neediest students, leaving them teary-eyed with gratitude for bringing them clarity, comfort, or hope.

At the end of the day, they lined up like devotees seeking a final audience with their guru. Harmony watched this as she put on her shoes and got ready to go. She was heading for the elevator when he called, "Harmony!"

"What?" she said without slowing her pace.

"Don't you say good-bye?"

"Good-bye," said Harmony.

"Wait a minute."

Harmony stopped with her back to him.

Joshua gestured "wait one second" to the student who was about to hug him. Then he stepped away from his post and walked over to Harmony, arms spread for a beneficent embrace.

Harmony knew exactly what he was doing, and allowed it. To the other students, he appeared to be a benevolent teacher giving a troubled, isolated hold-out an invitation to soften and connect. To Harmony, he was a master of energy circuitry showing off just how sly and knowing he was. With what looked like a paternal kiss to her forehead, he sent a laser beam of sexual energy down a direct line from Harmony's sixth chakra to her breasts and vagina, which spasmed with pleasure as his soft lips touched and sucked. Joshua was turned so that students waiting in line couldn't see his eyes. Only Harmony saw . . . and Grace, who at the moment of Harmony's orgasm, stepped out of the elevator right on time for her after-hours rendezvous with Joshua.

Chapter 29

HOSPITAL TALK

Harmony jolted awake at the electronic warble of the telephone. "Hello?" she croaked.

Cora said Joseph was still in New York Hospital, that he couldn't talk but was hysterical and had finally managed to write the letters H-A-R-M-O with his non-writing hand, which Walter Fortis took to mean that he wanted Harmony.

Cora had talked so fast it was hard to understand, and Harmony hoped she'd gotten the address right when, half an hour later, she looked at her scrawled note and hailed a cab. And she was halfway to the hospital before she remembered that she'd arranged to take today off.

By the time she arrived at Joseph's room on the sixth floor, Walter, who had been there all week, was downing his fourth cup of coffee and announcing to anyone who'd listen that Joseph was not his responsibility, they'd only dated for a few weeks, and he really had to get back to his own life.

Joseph was toupee-less and dressed in a hospital gown. Harmony didn't know where to look and her hands felt like foreign objects.

"Sit down," thought-talked Joseph, still with that glassy-eyed, vacant look.

Harmony carefully lowered herself onto the edge of the battered visitor's chair, wondering who was moaning and passing gas on the other side of the room divider. This was not how she'd intended to spend her vacation day. "So how are you feeling?" she queried politely.

"How the hell do you think?" thought-barked Joseph. "I can't talk or move, and I'm pissing through a tube!"

Harmony blushed and tried not to laugh.

"I need your help," continued Joseph. "I need you to listen very carefully and repeat back to me what I say so that I know you've heard correctly."

"Okay," thought-talked Harmony, and Joseph just stared. "I mean okay," she said out loud, realizing this was one-way telepathy. Good thing, since she was thinking how disgusting Joseph looked. His normal face tension had disappeared, revealing an inner expression that was hard to categorize—a kind of frozen, sunken sneer. Was it disdain or something more sinister? If Harmony were more experienced, she might have known, but all she knew was that she didn't like looking at him. So she focused on a place right above his eyes where there was no expression. "What do you want to tell me? I'll write it down," she said in a sudden burst of inspiration. If she were writing, she wouldn't have to look at him. She fished a pad and pen out of her purse and waited.

"I'm most likely going to die," thought-talked Joseph, matter-of-factly.

"Good god," gasped Harmony, "I'm sure that's not—"

"Shut up," ordered Joseph, and Harmony did. "Go to my apartment, find some papers, and take them to my lawyer. Will you do that?"

"Yes, I will go to your apartment and find some papers and take them to your lawyer," said Harmony out loud. She wondered what she was getting herself into and searched desperately for a way out. "Joseph, I don't think I can do this. Nobody is going to believe I'm acting on your instruc—"

"Shut up!" commanded Joseph. "I'll take care of that. The papers and lawyer information are in a file marked 'Emergency' in the desk in my bedroom. They contain a living will and a signed power of attorney. Repeat that please." And Harmony did. Joseph instructed her on where to find his keys and address and what to say to his doorman so that he'd let her in.

Joseph was giving off a pungent sour smell that Harmony couldn't identify. She felt bad that he was dying, but she rushed her good-bye in order to get out to clear air.

"Thank god," she sighed as she stepped into an empty elevator going down, and she breathed deeply for the first time in forty-five minutes. It was ten o'clock. If she got a cab right away, maybe she could finish Joseph's errands and still have some day left. She had an appointment with Dr. T at 6:30, and she wanted to go home first.

She was so busy wondering what Joseph's apartment would be like, and what she should say if anyone asked about Joseph, and if he didn't die, what he would say about their thought-talking once he could speak again, and if it would be so uncomfortable she'd finally have to quit her job, and if she did, how she'd make a living, that she almost didn't notice Joshua rushing past her in the lobby, half-carrying Frederic.

"Oh my god," she said, seeing him.

"Hi," said Joshua, and hurried on.

Chapter 30

JOSEPH'S SECRET

The elevator opened on the twenty-second floor of Joseph's Eastside high-rise. Harmony stepped out into a bare, beige hallway with brown industrial carpet. She tried to take up as little space as possible as she passed door after identical beige, metal door with chrome peepholes. No dogs barked behind them; no cats scratched; no babies cried. The place felt vacuum-packed.

Apartment 22N was the last one at the end of the last turn of the hallway. Harmony fumbled with the keys until she found the one that fit. "Hello? I hope nobody's here," she called as she opened the door. And she froze.

The living room looked like ghosts. The furniture was covered with white sheets that, on close inspection, appeared to be made of a cheap rayon mix. There were a few paint-by-numbers-type framed pictures of flowers in vases on the walls, and, although the windows faced south to make this an indoor gardener's heaven, there was not a living thing in sight. Not even a cactus.

A small door led out to a four-by-eight–foot terrace, also facing south, and the only sign that there had ever been plants was a neat stack of empty terra cotta pots. Although it was seventy degrees, Harmony shivered and closed the terrace door.

Joseph had said the papers were in the desk in his bedroom. Harmony walked down a narrow hall, past a closed door—a closet or a bathroom?—to another door. Closed doors seemed peculiar when you lived alone. But the authority of the closed bedroom door made her stop and knock. "Hello? I hope nobody's here," she called, nervously turning the knob.

In the center of the bedroom was a king-size bed that looked as if an economy-class motel maid had done her duty. There was an imitation oak nightstand with nothing on top of it, and a matching 1950s style desk.

The most remarkable thing about this whole apartment was the absence of stuff. Harmony envisioned Joseph's office and suddenly realized it was the same. There were copies of the magazine, work files, proofs, and the regular office equipment, but not one shred of anything personal. Just absence. The realization shocked her.

The desk had a middle drawer full of neatly compartmentalized paper clips, pens, pencils, and sundry stationery and supplies. One of the file-size side drawers was locked, and the other was open. She fingered through its Pendaflex file holders, neatly labeled in Joseph's block printing that for years had ordered her to REJECT or SEND FOR REV. or HOLD FOR CONSID.

HOLD FOR CONSID. meant that the submission would end up in a stack, eventually buried, the writer never acknowledged, finally lost—sort of like her in her managing editor job.

She didn't see any Pendaflexes with the word EMERGENCY, so she assumed the papers must be in the locked drawer. Joseph had said nothing about opening a locked drawer, and she didn't want to break into his private papers. She searched the house key ring, but there was no key small enough, which left two options: leave without completing the errand, or break the lock.

She tried twiddling the lock with an envelope opener, and when that didn't work, she poked through the crack between the drawer and body of the desk. When that didn't work, she footed the desk and yanked. There was a breaking sound and the drawer opened.

It looked just like the other drawer—more Pendaflex file holders with labels: APARTMENT LEASE, TAX RETURNS, INVESTMENTS, BOYS. Boys? Harmony got a sick feeling, but she pulled out the whole folder anyway. In it were several neatly labeled manila envelopes. Had they been sealed, she would have stopped. But they weren't.

"Aw, jeez!" she gasped as she stared at the contents of the first envelope. Then with heart-freezing recognition, "Oh, no! Aw, jeez; aw, jeez."

She was crying so hard she forgot to close the drawer or find the EMERGENCY file. She was sobbing so convulsively that she forgot she was in somebody else's apartment so you're not supposed to break their things or scream or wish them an agonizing, painful death. She cried as she ran out of the apartment, down twenty-two floors in the elevator, and she forgot to give Joseph's five dollar tip to the doorman or tell him she'd forgotten to lock the door. She cried as she leapt into a cab going south, and all the way downtown to her building and up the stairs to her apartment.

"Ruth," she gasped into the phone, still gripping the envelopes. "No, I'm fine. I just got home. Listen to me. I think I might have found your son."

At four o'clock, Cora called to say Joseph had died and don't bother to come in tomorrow because they were shutting editorial down until Quentin could reorganize the staff.

Harmony lit Joseph's five dollar bill with a wooden kitchen match and watched it burn. Then she threw the ash in the toilet and flushed twice.

Ruth met Harmony outside Dr. Thompson's building, and on seeing the photo, let loose a cry that sounded like it came from the bowels of the earth. Harmony held her until a minute before her appointment. And in any place other than New York City, people might have stopped and stared. But neither workers heading home from their jobs, nor dry cleaning boys on their last delivery, nor tourists looking for cheap restaurants even paused at the sight of the two women—one large black one and one of indeterminate race holding each other in a full-body embrace, weeping.

Chapter 31

JUDY

Judy had had it. Joshua had promised he'd be home at four o'clock to be with Emily so that Judy could go to her sister's piano recital. It was Lily's first New York performance, and Joshua knew how important this was. Instead, here was Judy at five minutes to five, too late to arrive on time even if Joshua *did* show up or decide to answer his cell phone. And what was worse—her therapist had said she was in denial—she knew he was with another woman.

"No," protested Joshua half an hour later. "Sweetheart, you've got it all wrong. It was Frederic. He thought he'd had a heart attack, I swear. He's exhausted, but I'm sure he'll tell you."

Judy paced and ground her teeth. "I'm sure he would confirm your story. I'm sure he'd say anything you told him to. I cannot take this anymore. It's humiliating. You said it would never happen again after that girl from the meditation retreat. You swore—"

"And I still do. On my life. Honestly, truly, there was no woman. Damn that quack you keep seeing! This is all her fault. I was at the hospital all day, and they tell you to turn off your cell. He called me at the office, and I took him to the hospital. I swear."

He was looking at her with such soft, sad, innocent eyes—those green eyes she'd fallen so in love with that it hurt. Judy longed to believe him. She longed to erase every intuition and suspicion. She longed to un-know every inkling, hint, and full-fledged sign: the hang-ups on their answering machine, the late nights when he "forgot" to turn on his cell phone, the chronic missed dinners. But she couldn't. "Joshua, I need you to leave," she said quietly.

"What?" he gasped. "Judy, please—"

"Just for a little while. I need you to go out for dinner. Just give me a few hours. I need to not see you for a while. Go to dinner and a movie. Can you do that for me?"

Joshua was scared. He wanted to hug Judy and make this go away, but he could feel her repulsion. He had felt her feel hurt, angry, and depressed, but never repulsed. He backed away, giving her space, checked his pockets for keys and money, and left.

Joshua rarely felt scared. He knew now was not the time, but he needed grounding, so he called Grace from the coffee shop around the corner from the school.

"Hi," he said when she answered.

"Joshua?" She sounded busy.

"Is this a bad time?"

There was a long pause. Oh god, thought Joshua. But he knew he deserved this.

"I can't do this anymore, Joshua," she said finally. "And neither can you."

"I know. I know," said Joshua penitently.

"No, I don't think you do know," continued Grace. "It's Harmony. I saw what you did, the way you looked at her after the last weekend. I didn't say anything because I didn't want to believe it was what it looked like. But I've had time to think, and I know what you're doing."

"What?"

"Don't say 'what.' I saw it, and I know what I saw. You gave her an orgasm. I don't know how, but somehow you did it by kissing her forehead. Do you have a death wish? You are playing with a time bomb. She's your student!"

"So I guess you don't want to meet for dinner and sex," said Joshua, suddenly feeling giddy, and Grace hung up.

Frederic was doing fine, said the floor nurse when Joshua phoned the hospital. He could go home tomorrow. Joshua promised to be there at nine o'clock to pick him up. He ate a cheeseburger—his first meat in ten years—went to a bad foreign movie at Frederic's revival house, and sat through it twice.

It was midnight when he slid into bed beside Judy. "Sweetheart?" he whispered, but she didn't answer.

On the Lower Eastside, Harmony tossed and cried out in her sleep. "No," she cried, "no!" She was in the car with her parents and they had just crashed into the tree. Her father was crushed against the steering wheel and her mother's head was covered with blood and shattered windshield glass. "No!" screamed Harmony, "Let me out!" Then suddenly everything went black, and somehow, even though she couldn't see her own hands, she knew she was locked in a closet. She screamed and screamed, but nobody could hear her. She screamed because she was scared, but also because it hurt. It hurt where she peed, and she was so scared. Then finally she couldn't scream anymore, so she just lay there in the black closet and waited to die.

She was too exhausted to make any noise or move when the door opened a crack letting in a sliver of white light, then suddenly light like the sun—a sun being, a being with light like the sun, and it was Joshua. He scooped her up in his strong arms, held her tight, and breathed life back into her through her forehead. "I can hear you, sweetheart," he whispered. "I can hear you."

And Harmony wrapped her legs around him and kissed him all over. She kissed his forehead, like he had done hers, and he arched in pleasure. Then she slid down his body, kissing down to his heart, and down and down.

"Harmony!" cried Joshua in his sleep, and very quietly, Judy slid out of bed, packed a few things, put Emily in her carriage, and left.

Chapter 32

DR. T

"How did you sleep?" asked Dr. Thompson, noting Harmony's puffy eyes and disheveled hair.

"Not great. Thanks for seeing me two days in a row," said Harmony. "Do you mind my drinking coffee during the session?"

"Not at all," said Dr. Thompson, sipping tea. "Why do you think I would mind?"

Harmony shrugged. Dr. Thompson drank tea at every session. "Just being polite, I guess."

"Do you feel you have to be polite to me?" queried Dr. Thompson, and Harmony gave her a withering look.

Harmony took a long sip of coffee, sloshing it around in her mouth to absorb the taste, then swallowed. "I guess I'm lucky not to be dead like Ruth's son. They'll probably never find him or whoever killed him. I can't believe I worked for a man who got off on pictures of mutilated dead boys." Harmony's stomach turned; she held up a finger for Dr. T to wait, then lurched for the bathroom.

When she got back, Dr. Thompson was still sipping tea.

Harmony ached all over, but the worst was in her groin. This was way different from the missile. This ache was bruising. She shifted, trying to relax down there. She couldn't remember her dreams, but she wondered if she'd hurt herself in her sleep.

"You look like you hurt," said Dr. Thompson. "How can I help?"

Dr. Thompson had always had a problem with her weight. She had thick, heavy legs that she was careful to keep covered, and an enormous behind that she tried to minimize with loose fitting skirts and over-blouses. As she asked Harmony the last question, she felt her entire lower half sink like a mountain into a suddenly shifting earth. Her legs rooted like giant redwoods. Such things happened when she was with Harmony, and she'd learned to go with them. "Harmony," she repeated, "tell me how I can help you."

Sometimes Harmony felt as if she were swirling hot energy with no body container. She felt Dr. T's weighty energy, and it felt good. Solid. Safe. Something to hold onto. "I'm not sure," she answered. "Don't leave."

"I'm not going anywhere," said Dr. Thompson, and Harmony felt a warm bubble from Dr. T's heart expand and surround her like a cocoon, and it felt good. "Would it be all right if I sat beside you?" asked Dr. Thompson, and Harmony nodded. She'd been afraid to ask.

Dr. Thompson set down her tea and rose slowly. Harmony had never noticed the true size of her behind. Her buttock cheeks rolled under her loose skirt, and the old couch shifted under her weight. "Can I touch you?" asked Dr. T, and Harmony said, "Please do."

Dr. Thompson put her warm hand on Harmony's forearm. Harmony's muscles turned to jelly and she collapsed into Dr. T's big, solid body and blubbered helplessly, "I can't. I can't."

"You can't what?" asked Dr. Thompson, rocking Harmony against her breast.

"I can't hold my head up."

"Then don't, sweetheart."

And Harmony sobbed with her whole body. Her baby arms flailed, her neck felt like rubber, and her legs like spaghetti. And Dr. Thompson held her and rocked.

After a while, Harmony couldn't make any more sounds, and Dr. Thompson stopped rocking and just held her.

"I hurt," said Harmony finally.

"I know," said Dr. Thompson.

"It's embarrassing where I hurt. It's like somebody killed me down there. I can't say it, but it hurts."

"I know," said Dr. Thompson, and she didn't need an explanation.

Later, after Harmony was able to sit up by herself and Dr. Thompson had moved back to her chair, Dr. T explained that sometimes we hold memories in our bodies that we have no stories for, but feeling the memories is the beginning of feeling better.

Harmony told Dr. T that even though Joshua was a womanizing dick, he was the first man she'd ever felt safe with, and sometimes she missed him so much she thought it might kill her. She didn't know if this meant she was "in love." And Dr. T said maybe she could just call it love and not worry about what kind. Harmony said that sounded good and apologized for crying all over Dr. T's linen blouse, and Dr. T said not to worry about it.

Harmony asked if Dr. T thought it was screwed up to want to see Joshua so much she was willing to pay tuition to be taught by incompetent students, and Dr. T said no. Maybe Harmony should just enjoy loving someone, no matter what it looked like. That made Harmony feel good. She valued Dr. T's opinion, and she decided she wouldn't quit the school, but the expense of therapy on top of tuition was difficult, so could they wait a month for their next session.

They scheduled an appointment for April, following the school weekend, and Harmony hugged Dr. T good-bye.

Chapter 33

REPRISE OF THE COCKROACH IN REAL TIME

"You think if you don't move, I won't kill you," murmured Joshua. "And don't pretend you don't understand me." . . .

After Joshua chased the cockroach into the wall; after his and Harmony's energy sex; after a bug crawled out of Harmony's bathroom wall and war was officially declared, Harmony felt much better. Lighter. Relieved!

She resumed sessions with Kathy Smith and even added a "tone and sculpt" class where Kathy taught something called "the plank"—a horrible pose where you balanced on your toes and your elbows until you collapsed. It was supposed to strengthen your "core" and, although Harmony doubted she had one, since most of the time she felt like a mass of seething energy that one day might self-immolate, she did her best. "Damn you, Kathy Smith!" she yelled as she gripped and balanced. "Nobody can do this damned exercise! I hate you!" And then she laughed when Kathy just smiled and assured her that she was doing very, very well and in just five more seconds, it would be over.

Despite her loathing of the plank, Harmony did it every day for the three weeks she had off from work; Quentin was looking for a new editor-in-chief and had suspended production of *Your Garden* for one issue with everyone on half-salary. In addition to getting in shape, Harmony used the time to fix up her own little indoor garden. She bought the expensive humidifying and air filtration system advertised in *Your Garden* to transform any indoor space into a greenhouse, in the hope that it would encourage the orchids to bloom. She washed all the *dracaenas* and every leaf of her ficus tree. She used a soft shoe-polishing brush to clean the fuzzy leaves of her African violets and she cut back the geraniums and started new plants from the cuttings. She root pruned her night-blooming jasmine so it could stay in its pot and grow thick and bushy, and she rearranged the animals in her bedroom water garden into pairs: the glow-in-the-dark frogs on top of each other in a suggestive position; the snakes wound around the tiny monkeys; and the angry troll, whose raised arms once protested life, was now offering up a miniature watermelon. It took half an hour with Superglue to get the bluebird lighting on the melon as if it were taking a bite.

Although she couldn't envision herself making a daily hike to Avenue B and Sixth Street, Harmony decided to take one more look at the community garden. This time she heard it from half a block away—a boom box blasting the Pointer Sisters singing "Jump." Weren't there regulations about amplified music in public spaces?

The gate was unlocked and the place was bustling with activity: crouching, bending, cutting-and-hauling people moved about like a tribe of worker ants scurrying to the soundtrack of "Jump!" It made sense that they would be cleaning out dead stuff just before spring, and the song was catchy: Jump! dah-dah-dah-dah-da-da . . . As she watched through the iron fence posts, Harmony realized how little she knew about outdoor gardening. "Jump! dah-dah-dah-dah-da-da!" Perhaps she would buy a CD and add it to her dance collection.

"Do you wanna come in?" bellowed a heavy-set woman for the second time. In response, Harmony waved and mouthed that she couldn't hear anything. The woman, strode forward; she looked like one of the take-charge assistants at the Healing School. Perhaps there really were a limited amount of personality and body types and all groups had representatives from the same pool.

"I said come in!" yelled the woman from middle of the garden—this time it was an order. "We can use all the hands we can get."

Even though she had no intention of working, let alone trying to join another group, Harmony obediently entered through the unlocked gate.

"Are you new?" demanded the woman, as Harmony approached.

"I'm not a member," said Harmony. "I was just looking. It's hard to hear."

"Oh. Well dues are five dollars to become a FOG—friend of the garden, then after we get to know you, you can apply for a plot. This puts you on our mailing list, so that you find out about garden meetings and events and such. You become a full member when you receive a plot. Plots are given out as they become available to FOGs selected by the Membership Committee *at its sole discretion*. The music inspires us." She sounded as if she'd memorized this.

"I-was-just-looking!" yelled Harmony politely. It was impossible not to talk on the beat.

"Hank over there can use some help with the mulch. Gloves are in the wheel barrow. Make yourself useful," ordered the woman.

Hank? Harmony rolled her eyes.

"Do you have a problem?" demanded the woman.

"No, no. I'm sorry. I was thinking of something else. By the way, I'm Harmony."

"Swell," said the woman. "Oh, and you really should know, volunteer hours in the garden may help your chances of getting a plot. Just ask garden members and heads of committees about their needs and projects. Everything's by committee."

"Nice," said Harmony, twisting her mouth into what she hoped was a smile but making no move toward the wheel barrow.

"Once you become a member, we expect you to garden and maintain your plot, to give four hours of service per month to the garden, to attend monthly garden meetings, and to abide by garden rules. We take these membership conditions seriously. Be sure you can make this kind of commitment. Chop-chop. Jump in! The mulch doesn't move itself."

"Listen," said Harmony as nicely as she could, "I appreciate all the information. I'll be in touch." And as she about-turned to make a speedy exit, she noticed an Asian man in what looked like maroon robes squatting in front of a leaf-covered plot with a small stone Buddha statue under a tree, to the left of the exit. A monk? Harmony smiled. Although she'd never articulated it, the profession appealed to her.

"Hi," he said, rising to her height as she passed on her way to the gate.

"Hi."

"You'd fit in here," he said, winking.

He was dark, short for a guy, in his fifties or sixties—hard to tell. Was he Asian or part-Black? Harmony couldn't believe she was wondering about race. And his eyes seemed to point in different directions. "I'm just looking," she yelled over the Pointer Sisters. "I've never done outdoor gardening."

"You'll learn," said the monk, and even though he spoke in a normal tone of voice, Harmony heard him quite clearly. "Everybody does eventually," he said, stuffing a handful of leaves into a plastic garbage bag.

Harmony froze, watching him shove another armload of leaves into the bag. "Jump!" sang the Pointer Sisters.

"Rinpoche!" hollered the woman with the big voice. "The mulch goes in the damn mulch pile not in the garbage! How many times do I have to tell you?"

"Sorry," called Rinpoche, suppressing a smile and dumping the leaves back onto his plot. Then effortlessly he dropped into a squat and resumed his work.

As Harmony walked home, she sang softly: Jump dah-dah-dah-dah-da-da. And while she sang, she mused: Kathy Smith could use some Pointer Sisters in her videos. The canned music was a little sterile. But even so, Kathy Smith was wonderful—so kind when she assured you that you could do five more seconds of a torturous exercise. What was a Buddhist Rinpoche doing in a community garden? Jump! dah-dah-dah-dah-da-da . . . He might well be the most relaxed person she'd ever seen in the face of loud-voiced harsh words bellowed over an earsplitting soundtrack. What if the opposite of Kathy Smith's plank was the way the Rinpoche smiled and almost seemed amused by the loud-voiced woman? And how on earth did you get that relaxed? Dr. T had recommended planting your feet for grounding. That Rinpoche had to be deep breathing—another way to deal with unpleasant sensations. She would talk to Dr. T about this. And just as she was thinking this, a huge cockroach skittered across the sidewalk in front of her.

"Jump," she sang, nimbly sidestepping, and, remembering her energy sex orgasm, she blushed.

Chapter 34

BALANCE/IMBALANCE

By April's healing weekend, Harmony was so hot and aroused she feared that one look from Joshua would throw her into an orgasm. She sat upright on her chair with her bare feet planted on the floor the way Dr. T had advised, and she practiced the opposite of the plank by deep breathing like the Rinpoche. The class shifted restlessly, waiting for Joshua. He was ten minutes late and people had begun chatting. Harmony never cared for chatter, but she tried to listen nonjudgmentally. The thought of Joshua had launched an energy streamer through her uterus and she felt her face flush. She wondered if it was noticeable to the others. She wondered if Joshua would acknowledge what they had been doing—since he'd initiated at least half of their exchanges, it was clearly a reciprocal affair.

"So what's cooking?" said Joshua from the doorway, and everyone hushed. He smiled so his eyes lit up, but Harmony was shocked. Was she imagining it or was his beautiful dark brown hair now speckled with gray and was there a pale and drawn quality hiding behind his smiling eyes? She felt deeper, then pulled back at his energetic rebuff, although he still hadn't looked in her direction. She glanced at the other students, but everyone was smiling as though nothing were different. That's the thing about idealizing someone. When you turn them into a "thing" to be adored, you wipe out their pain. But Joshua didn't look like a really pissed off lab rat. He still looked like a movie star, a fox—albeit a silver one—but, despite the distinguished appearance, something wasn't right. As he walked through the center of the circle to his chair, Harmony softened the front of her body to feel him, and zap came a pain that felt like heartbreak in her mid-section. She clasped her hands over the area and tried to soothe it. What the hell was going on?

"So how was everyone's month?" asked Joshua, relaxing into his chair and patting the knees of the assistants on either side of him as if he hadn't turned into another person.

Hank, who looked like a six-year-old ready to burst, exploded into a story about how his old lover who'd dumped him for a rock star had called begging Hank to take him back. Then he paused for dramatic effect.

"So did you?" asked Joshua.

"Of course not. He dumped me."

"So you assume it could never work again?"

Hank looked confused, his pride in his assertiveness suddenly suspect. "Well, I talked about it to my therapist, and we agreed—"

"Your therapist," interrupted Joshua. "How long have you been with this therapist?"

"Fifteen years," said Hank, nonplused.

Joshua laughed. "Let me guess. For fifteen years you've talked about your childhood—how your father rejected you, your mother tried to seduce you, and because of this you can't maintain a significant relationship. Now the one man you've ever really loved has begged you to take him back, and your therapist has advised you against it."

Hank nodded, speechless.

"How much do you pay this therapist?" demanded Joshua.

"One hundred thirty dollars a session," answered Hank softly.

"So let me see—I can't even calculate what you've paid this woman. It is a woman, isn't it?"

Hank nodded.

"Of course," said Joshua disdainfully. "I hate this. I just hate this kind of dependence. I want you all to hear this. Hank, tell the class how much your relationship issues have changed in the fifteen years you've been seeing this therapist—once a week, is it?"

"Except when she goes away," said Hank sheepishly.

"Right! When *she* goes away, you stop. But I bet *you* can't cancel an appointment."

"Sure, I can," protested Hank. "As long as I give forty-eight hours' notice."

Joshua rolled his eyes. "So, have you changed? Tell the class."

Hank blushed, stared at the floor, and mouthed something.

"What? Can you answer louder? We can't hear you."

"No!" shouted Hank.

"So for fifteen years, you've paid this woman to rehearse your problems. She has you caught in a symbiotic web of dependence. She keeps you complaining, which reinforces your belief in your problems, so you're convinced that you need her. And she is dependent on you for her income. My god, you've probably paid for several country houses! How I hate this. The therapeutic community with their Ph.Ds. and diagnoses should be junked. The only way to change is to accept your own greatness. Did everyone hear that? I'll say it again." And he did.

The class sat in stunned silence.

Harmony looked from face to face and what she saw was shame on the faces of those who were in therapy and a kind of superior gloat on those who were not. She wanted somebody to protest.

"Excuse me," she said when she could no longer stand it. And the sudden focus of everyone's eyes on her made her blush. "I don't think all therapy is bad or that all therapists should be junked. I'm sure there are some situations where there's an unhealthy dependence, but I think you're making a very wrong generalization."

Joshua glared at her. She could feel his fire, and it didn't feel sexy. "Are you in therapy?" he asked.

"As a matter of fact, I am."

"Do you feel your therapist is helping you to have a stronger grasp of reality?"

What a puzzling question. "Yes, I do."

Joshua pondered this.

"And I don't think she's doing it just for the money."

"I never said—"

"Yes, you did," interrupted Harmony. "You said therapists create a symbiotic dependence because they need the income. I wonder if there might be some projection since you've got something like that going on right here."

Several students gasped and looked like they wanted to punch her.

"No, let her go on. I want to hear this," said Joshua, smiling and gesturing for people to be quiet.

Harmony shifted uncomfortably and tried to plant her feet better. "I think you've created the very dependence you say you hate. You've got all these people—these student assistant teachers—totally dependent on you as the only authority. In fact, nobody even questioned what you said about therapists because they believe everything you say is gospel. And you are financially dependent on them because they're teaching half the classes for free! This is how cults come about." Harmony tried her best to breathe, but no air would move.

A furious mumble erupted among the assistants; the other students looked confused; and Joshua stared.

"I just don't think you can make generalizations about everyone in a profession, that's all." Harmony slid back in her chair and slumped down. She wanted to end this. She wanted to breathe. But Joshua stared and waited. "We all need to trust somebody in order to heal; you said that nobody can do it in isolation. All I'm saying is that there are some very good therapists. I think I'm going to faint." As she slumped and Joshua stared, she thought-talked one last thing: "Who do *you* ask for help?"

There was a long, uneasy silence. Then Joshua announced that today the class would be going over the endocrine system because in order to understand how you function, you need to understand your glands.

Endocrine balancing was like the regular table work, said Joshua, but instead of dealing with chakras, you envisioned the various glands—adrenals, ovaries or testes, pancreas, thymus, thyroid and parathyroid, hypothalamus and pituitary, and finally the pineal which was the link to Divine Consciousness. You touch them with the intention to invite their intelligence into its fullest functioning.

Then he explained what each of the glands related to. Even though Harmony hated taking notes and had given up all thoughts of becoming a professional healer, she drew a chart:

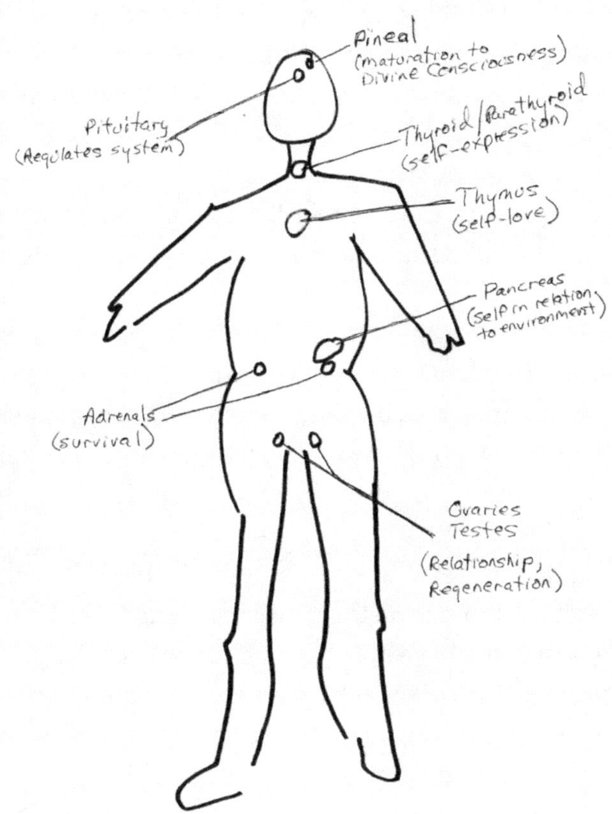

She studied her picture and, after some contemplation, concluded that she and Joshua had matching ovaries/testes imbalances, so their relationship was indeed mutually healing. When students paired for the table work endocrine balancing exercise, she volunteered to be Hank's healer, much to his surprise. She did it because he was a man. And Joshua was a man. And if it is true that we are all one, then maybe by working on Hank, she could somehow help Joshua.

"Right hand between the legs—no touching," instructed Joshua, and several people laughed. "And left hand on the second chakra."

Harmony wasn't used to having her hand between a man's legs, but she tried to pretend this was Joshua. And suddenly there was no problem. Hank smiled, but Harmony ignored it, concentrating on the huge ball of light that faded up into brightness just above his pelvis.

"Imagine a light body above the pelvis," instructed Joshua. "It's where the two adrenals merge into one. Invite it into wholeness."

Harmony watched with amazement as the ball grew brighter and pulsed.

"Now keeping your right hand where it is, move your left to the third chakra at the bottom of the sternum."

The pelvic ball grew to the size of a beach ball and changed from red to orange. Harmony felt like she was in an amusement park as it danced and pulsed.

"You're inviting the ovaries or testes into fullness," said Joshua. "See the person in their light body—"

And Harmony stopped hearing Joshua and only heard music—like a chorus of angels, only they were singing a show tune: "He won't dance. Don't ask him." Like in her vision of the three black women. Harmony bit her tongue to keep from laughing.

Joshua suddenly felt weak. There was a jolt in his pelvis, then a hot stirring of his insides, almost as if there were internal bleeding, except it felt good. Exciting. It felt like his whole life was inside his pelvis, and as his knees buckled, he grabbed for the nearest support, but there was none. He was standing alone next to nothing. And the last thing he saw before passing out was Harmony playing with a red-orange ball of light.

"Do you want us to call Judy?" said one of the worried assistants surrounding Joshua.

"No, no. What happened?" he said, struggling to sit up.

"Keep him down," said someone to Martha, the lead assistant, as though Joshua couldn't hear.

"I'm going to call Judy," said Martha.

Joshua sat up. "I said, no! I'm fine. Somebody get me a glass of water."

Three assistants battled each other to obey, and Martha went for the water.

"I'm fine. It's nothing to worry about, but thank you all for your concern," said Joshua warmly, but clearly dismissing his attendants. He drank the water and told the class he needed to eat, so they would break early for lunch. The assistants he usually lunched with waited expectantly, but he ignored them. "Harmony," he called, "I want to talk to you in my office."

Something in his tone sent fear through Harmony, but she said sure, and followed him out the little side door behind the sound system.

"You are very talented. You have a lot of gifts," said Joshua. He and Harmony were sitting side-by-side on his small leather couch, and Harmony could feel his heat.

"Thank you," she said. "So do you."

Joshua searched for just the right words. He didn't want to make a mistake. "Sometimes it's possible to misuse your gifts, either unintentionally or intentionally." He paused, watching for a reaction. Harmony looked blank. "When you have strong energy, you have increased responsibility about how you use it."

Harmony was puzzled. "Are you talking about what I said earlier about therapy or what I did in the endocrine balancing exercise?"

"So you acknowledge it!" Joshua laughed. He'd assumed he would hit denial. Maybe this would be easier than he'd thought.

"Of course, I acknowledge it," said Harmony. "Why wouldn't I acknowledge what I did? You and I have the same problem with relationships, only we deal with it in opposite ways, so I thought maybe we could help each other."

Joshua crossed his legs. "What problem is that?"

Harmony wondered if he was joking. "We isolate."

"This is what you think?"

"Yes," said Harmony, getting an uncomfortable feeling. "And you said the ovaries and testes are in charge of relationship, so I thought I could help when I worked on Hank. And I think what we've been doing with each other is probably just the right thing to help both of us."

"And what have we been doing?"

"The sex!" said Harmony, incredulous. "The energy sex."

"Excuse me?" said Joshua, and Harmony felt sick.

"Look, you don't have to deny it. We haven't done anything wrong."

"There's nothing to deny," said Joshua in a smooth-voiced monotone so cold and fake warm that Harmony's arm hairs stood on end.

"Are you saying nothing has been going on between us?" she asked, feeling a little faint.

"I can only speak for myself," said Joshua, "and I know nothing is going on for me. Harmony, you don't even know me. It's all fantasies."

And Harmony felt the back of her head explode, letting out all her life energy.

Chapter 35

CRAZY

"Do you think I'm crazy?" demanded Harmony for the second time.

Dr. Thompson decided to go with her gut. "I don't think you're crazy. I don't really understand what Joshua is doing, but I believe you experienced what you say you experienced."

Harmony thought about this. "But do you think what I experienced was real?"

"I believe it was real for you."

This was the answer Harmony had been dreading. "Oh god," she moaned, covering her face with her hands. "Oh my god."

"What?" said Dr. Thompson.

"You don't believe me."

"I didn't say that."

"What if I am crazy? What if my whole life I've been crazy and nothing I've experienced is real?" Harmony felt as if she were being electrocuted from the inside out. Her arm hairs were standing on end and there was ice water in her veins. "Isn't the sign that you're crazy that you don't think you are? All my life I've been absolutely certain of what I feel and what I know, and I felt and knew that Joshua and I were having energy sex. He penetrated me. He visited me in dreams, and he said I was driving him crazy! What if I'm out of my mind and none of this ever happened?"

"Can you look at me, Harmony?" said Dr. Thompson.

Harmony realized she'd almost forgotten Dr. T was in the room. "Yes, of course. How rude of me."

"Can you see me?"

"Not so well." Her vision was fuzzy and she felt a little foggy. "My feet. It's my feet, right?" She kicked off her shoes and planted.

"And how about breathing?"

"Yes, okay, breathing is good. I wanted to talk to you about that anyway. I—"

"If you stop talking, this might be easier."

"Sure. Of course." Harmony shut up and breathed, and gradually Dr. Thompson came into focus and Harmony started feeling clearer, calmer. "I like air," she said, after a minute.

Dr. Thompson studied her. She looked like she was all here now. "Harmony, I have no way of knowing whether what you experienced was real. All I can know is what you tell me. Tell me. Was it real?"

Harmony didn't even have to think. "Yes," she answered. "Absolutely, yes."

"So that's got to be good enough. Can that be good enough?"

Harmony stared at her planted feet. She stared at her shoes. They were red. She liked them. "I guess so," she said softly. "Yes."

"You certainly look better when you accept your own truth," said Dr. Thompson, marveling at the sudden change in Harmony's complexion. The minute she'd said yes, all the tension had disappeared and she'd become so beautiful. Harmony was an unusually beautiful woman.

"Thanks," said Harmony, and they both laughed.

"Why do you think he denied it?" asked Dr. Thompson after a while.

Harmony shrugged. "I think he's lonelier than I am. And I think he loves me. And it scares him."

"Okay," said Dr. Thompson. "The hour's up. Just stay with what you know."

"See you next month," said Harmony.

"Call if you need to."

Chapter 36

ENDINGS

Joshua had called Frederic every day since he'd brought him home from the hospital; he'd brought him organic oranges, whole-grain breads, and magazines; he did subtle clearings of Frederic's heart chakra, boosted his thymus, and never mentioned that Judy had left with the baby and Grace wasn't speaking to him.

He was making amazing, albeit subtle, progress with Georgie, his autistic boy, but Georgie's mother couldn't detect or appreciate it. And since he was bound by confidentiality, there was nobody he could share the details with. If he'd had close professional colleagues, he could have talked about it as a case study, but although he was well-known in the healing community, Joshua worked alone. He'd stopped attending other people's workshops years ago, so his main contact was with his students and clients. He'd given up leaving messages for Judy on her sister's answering machine. He considered contacting an attorney about Emily, but since he was in no position to take care of her, he thought it best to wait for Judy to cool down and contact him about visitation.

After a while, Frederic got tired of Joshua's solicitousness and asked him to take a break.

Joshua nearly doubled his private sessions with clients and he joined a gym.

Your Garden Magazine was folding. It was a horrible shock. Harmony got an email that there would be a final staff meeting with Quentin to explain the details.

"I want you all to know that this was an absolutely wrenching decision. We did not come to it easily," said Quentin from the podium in the cavernous publisher's ballroom, normally used for Christmas parties. Quentin looked like Superman actor Christopher Reeve before his accident. Several of the women joked that all he needed was a cape.

Suddenly overcome with the vision of Quentin and Joseph in bed, Harmony cringed and stared at the floor.

"Are you okay?" whispered Cora who was now wig-less, with beautiful short blonde curls.

Harmony nodded, breathed deeply, and circled her fingers in an "okay" sign.

"Although we all will sorely miss Joseph Timiani, the ending of *Your Garden* is in no way connected to his passing," continued Quentin. He explained that subscriptions were down by a third since last year and newsstand sales had tanked due to a glut of similar magazines. The board of the publishing conglomerate had therefore decided to kill *Your Garden* and concentrate in other markets. Then, thanking everyone for their dedication and service, Quentin left the podium.

Grace took the stage and explained that everyone would receive their last paycheck in full as a gesture of gratitude, but since the company was being dissolved, there would be no extended benefits.

A stunned silence filled the ballroom. They were a small staff that seemed even smaller clumped together in this enormous vacant space. Several of the older editors who had been at the magazine since its inception forty years ago, began to cry, but not too loudly.

"Well, I guess that's that," said Cora, matter-of-factly. "Good thing I got cancer while I still had medical coverage."

"Do you want to go back to the office to get our stuff?" asked Harmony. "I'm going to need a cab to get all my plants home. I hope they're still alive. I don't even know where you live."

"In the Village," said Cora. "Sure, let's go."

"Which Village?" asked Harmony, realizing how little she knew about this woman she'd work with for over five years.

"East," said Cora.

"Me, too!" said Harmony.

"That's nice."

Harmony didn't mind that Cora didn't ask what street. Maybe it wasn't all

Harmony's fault that they didn't connect. Maybe closeness was determined by belly cords rather than proximity.

One of the cleaning staff had watered the plants, so they were still alive. Harmony was relieved. The anemic philodendron would be much happier in a Lower Eastside apartment with a somewhat obstructed southern exposure. It could hang near the kitchen and still get enough light. Harmony wound its long stems around the pot and gently lowered it into a shopping bag. The rubber tree was almost ready to propagate, and she would prefer to make the trunk incision—covered by rooting hormone, sphagnum moss, and a plastic bag—at home where she wouldn't be asked what she was doing. She put Joseph's orchid near the trash with a "Thank you for watering. Please Take Me" sign on it. Maybe the plant-loving cleaner would rescue it. It needed somebody who didn't know its lineage. And what to do with the dead-looking snake plant? She stuck her finger down in the soil—no root rot; that was a good sign. The remaining leaves cracked off as she touched them. On an impulse, she stuck the pot in the bag with the philodendron. Maybe if she waited, new leaves would come.

Harmony and Cora shared a cab downtown, and Cora insisted on getting out at National Wholesale Liquidators because she just had to purchase some discount home-care products. Harmony still didn't know where Cora lived. "Well, maybe we'll see each other sometime," she said.

"Sure," said Cora, handing her some money for the cab. And she was gone.

Harmony felt sad as she climbed the stairs to her apartment. She was glad the job was over. She had never felt comfortable with Cora, and although she wasn't happy Joseph had died, she wasn't sad that he was dead. She just felt sad.

Despite what had happened with Joshua, she was glad she hadn't quit the school because at least there was somewhere she was committed to going.

She supposed she should start looking for another job, but her apartment was rent stabilized and she had some savings. Maybe next week she'd visit that plant store she liked in Chelsea and see if they needed help. It would be minimum wage, but the atmosphere was nice. Also, it wasn't far from the healing school, and it might be nice to work in Joshua's neighborhood.

Next to houseplants, Harmony's favorite thing was music, and in particular, Broadway musicals. Although she knew she shouldn't spend money on non-essentials, she bought a CD of *Carousel* with Barbara Cook that she listened to every day for weeks.

There were so many wonderful songs on it: "If I Loved You," "What's the Use of Wond'rin," and no matter how many times she listened, she was reduced to a puddle by "You'll Never Walk Alone." When she wanted to dance, she made sure her curtains were closed and then put on the overture—"The Carousel Waltz"—loud, on repeat-play.

"The Carousel Waltz" started so eerily it sounded like something awful was going to happen, but then it segued into gliding, floating, soaring melody. Harmony found herself leaping onto chairs and twirling on her way back down to the floor. Sometimes she'd pretend she was a figure skater or a ballerina, and when the living room got too small, she'd spin into the bedroom. She pretend-waltzed with a partner, dipping and turning, and sometimes she could almost see her father throwing back his head and laughing like he was Gene Kelly. And sometimes it was Joshua.

Sometimes she'd close her eyes and twirl until she didn't know which way was up, and she felt like she was flying or falling—it didn't matter which. She spread her arms like an angel with wings and let it happen.

Chapter 37

CHARACTEROLOGY

Harmony didn't speak during the morning session of the first May class, and Joshua barely looked her way. He said they would be learning about the German physician Wilhelm Reich's five character types, doing one a month through September. Although Joshua didn't believe in diagnosing people, he found the characterology—which was based on how people defend when they feel threatened—helpful for bringing your unconscious behaviors into awareness. He said everybody was a mix of types, but you might recognize one or two as your predominant ways of coping. Because this sounded interesting, Harmony took notes:

> <u>Schizoid</u>. Person doesn't feel safe. Feels separate, more special than others or more defective. They are afraid of connection— eye contact, physical touch, etc. The defense is to "split"—energy leaves the body through leaks in the joints or through the top of the head—sometimes causing a "disjointed" appearance. Best to approach from an oblique angle—never face to face. Many people with schizoid defense have vision problems due to constriction in the occipital lobe—with particular problems seeing faces. May have access to the divine, but they don't know how to relate to others and are often perceived as arrogant. As a result, they are half-people, believing they are in touch with something greater, but never truly experiencing it, because true divinity comes through loving another. They are neither here nor there. It's tragic.

Harmony smoothed her uneven hair and tried to listen to the next three types—oral, masochist, and rigid—but she was too "split" to take notes. No matter. She'd get the information in the weekends that followed. But she tuned in for number five, psychopath:

> <u>Psychopath</u>. Must maintain control. They do it through force, manipulation, or seduction.

Harmony sat upright and watched Joshua, who continued lecturing as if he were talking about someone else.

> In the quest for control, the psychopath distorts the truth. The way to help someone with such a defense is to stay in truth, no matter how the psychopath attempts to manipulate. The psychopath can look any which way. They are generally attractive and charming, and since they succeed in life, they rarely go to anyone for help. But they never achieve what they really want— to be known and valued for who they really are.

Joshua left the room and his main assistant, Martha, led the class in this month's exercise to clarify the schizoid experience. It had to do with reliving what it felt like to be a baby rejected by its mother. Martha instructed half of the class to be babies and half to be mean mothers. Harmony was put in the babies' group, but she'd learned about following student teachers' instructions, so when Martha said in a hypnotic voice, "You are now two weeks old," Harmony sat bolt upright and decided to observe instead of participate. Her mean mother partner got upset, and Harmony told her to go to hell.

Then she left the room—to do what, she didn't know. She had no intention of leaving; she wasn't feeling nuts; she just wanted to get out of the room and breathe. She was looking out the window between the men's and women's bathrooms when she heard singing: the opening to "Mr. Snow" from *Carousel*. What a coincidence.

The sliding door to Joshua's private bathroom opened and there stood Joshua looking at her with those glittering eyes that sent her into something that felt like either ecstasy or terror.

"I didn't know there was a room behind that wall," blurted Harmony. "And I didn't know you could sing. That's from *Carousel*, isn't it?"

Joshua shrugged and kept looking at her. Harmony felt warm, tingly energy touch her heart, then envelop her—like the gentlest hug, holding every inch, every cell of her body in tenderness. She closed her eyes and melted, and all there was was that tenderness, that love. But when she opened her eyes, all she saw was Joshua's back as he headed for the other classroom, singing about if somebody loved somebody.

I guess he likes *Carousel* too, thought Harmony, knowing this had nothing to do with what had just happened.

Chapter 38

SPEAKING TRUTH

June, July, and August Harmony's class studied the oral, masochist, and rigid character structures and relived the original wounds—abandonment, domination, and rejection by the opposite sex parent—in assistant-led exercises.

The oral abandonment exercise did not involve partners; class members would pretend to be solo babies and, at the start, Harmony had simply explained to the lead assistant, Martha, that, on her very experienced doctor's instructions, she would observe from a chair rather than defer to neophyte student teachers.

"Please lie on your backs in a circle," Martha instructed the rest of the class. "Heads on the inside."

Planting her bare feet on the floor, Harmony watched with a willfully detached slack mouth while deep breathing and creating an angry red whip line on her wrist by snapping a rubber band—a technique she'd learned from a panic attack website. So what if Martha couldn't understand. Dr. T had suggested that fully participating in exercises where she re-lived infancy might be counterproductive. Most people have difficulty accessing feelings or going into altered states, Dr. T had explained, and since Harmony went wacko (Harmony's words, not Dr. T's) without effort, it might be best if she concentrated on being in the here and now, thereby observing any strong emotions that might arise with some objectivity. Dr. T said that it took a lot of experience for teachers and therapists to understand the different needs of students and clients, and probably student teachers wouldn't know this.

As Roger, the other assistant, slowly dimmed the lights, Martha began the story of feeling hungry:

"You are a little baby and you feel warm and cozy in your little crib in your little room."

Snap went the rubber band and Harmony smiled pleasantly at Martha's dirty look.

"You love being a baby," prompted Martha, and Harmony covered her mouth and tried not to laugh as the whole circle of full-sized adults squirmed and gurgled and some even sucked their thumbs. A few, like Sherry and Roxana, seemed to take it very seriously, while others, like Hank, seemed to be performing for an unseen audience. In fact, several times Hank broke character to glance around and gauge how he was doing compared to the other babies.

Harmony choked an inchoate laugh—something in Hank's expression stopped it. It was only a second, but as he realized everybody else was doing their best to pretend to be a baby, and here he was all alone worrying about how his performance stacked up, Hank's face fell apart.

The room was dim and Harmony was out of his view. As she watched his despair turn to self-loathing, her heart cracked and it was all she could do to keep from yelling, "You're not alone! I'm watching too. It's no big deal. It's just pretend."

"Now you're starting to feel an uncomfortable feeling in your tummy," murmured Martha in her best soothing voice.

And Harmony watched Martha. She sounded so self-assured, so mature, but something in her body contradicted this. Harmony had never noticed how caved in Martha's chest was. She had a nice body with full breasts, but her posture was funny—caved in and forced forward at the same time—as if she were terrified but trying to hide it by forcing her shoulders back to show off her breasts.

As Harmony watched, she felt Martha's shame of her fear, and it was all she could do to keep from yelling, "You're not alone! I'm scared too!"

"You're hungry," directed Martha more forcefully, "and you begin to cry for your mother."

And the circle of big adults began to whimper and cry—first softly, and then with growing desperation, as no mothers came. And suddenly Harmony, who was spontaneously breathing deeper than she had ever breathed before and desperately lashing her wrist with the rubber band, didn't feel like laughing.

July was masochist month, and since domination wasn't really Harmony's issue, she did that exercise. Sherry played her bully mother, and when Sherry tried to overpower Harmony, Harmony told her to fuck off.

Martha praised Harmony and said that was an appropriate reaction to be being bullied. Harmony was pleased. But then she saw Sherry's expression. It lasted only a second, but it was like a fast-motion movie of surprise, hurt, rage, and finally shame. Harmony felt how helpless Sherry felt, how good it had been to feel stronger than somebody else, how hurt she was at being so rudely and unexpectedly rebuffed by someone half her size, and how mortified she was that she had enjoyed being a bully. And it was all Harmony could do to keep from hugging her and saying, "Me, too!" But she knew that Sherry would have let loose a mildew stink, resenting Harmony for seeing what she believed was hidden. She would have cackled disdainfully and said Harmony was imagining things; that after all, unlike Harmony, Sherry was a mother and certainly would never take pleasure in bullying anyone.

Since there weren't any men besides Hank for August's rigid exercise, Harmony and several other women got to be rejecting fathers—which Harmony rather enjoyed. Nobody playing children seemed to get upset. The ones without rigid issues felt silly pretending to be upset that a woman pretending to be a man was turning her back on them. And the people with rigid issues were far too rigid to feel hurt.

"You liked that, huh?" said Joshua afterwards. Sometimes he dropped in at the end of exercises and observed from the doorway. The class had broken up, and Harmony was surprised to be alone, sans the regular crowd of Joshua-admirers.

"It was okay," she answered.

"You like rejecting people?"

"Not particularly. It was a new experience. Usually I'm the rejectee, if that's a word."

"You seem to have disappeared in the last few months."

"What do you mean? I've come to class," said Harmony, feigning ignorance by checking her sleeve for lint.

"Okay," said Joshua.

Harmony swallowed. She was not going to get caught reacting to something that he would later deny. "I've been unemployed," she said, apropos of nothing.

"I'm sorry," said Joshua. "You know, I hardly know anything about you. You never share anything personal in class."

"Neither do you."

"That's because I'm the teacher," said Joshua, without missing a beat.

"Oh, is that it?" said Harmony. "It's very empty being unemployed. Almost as empty as my job felt."

"I'm sorry to hear that," said Joshua. "Maybe you need work that's more fulfilling."

"Maybe so," said Harmony. "I'm forty-three years old."

Joshua shrugged, suddenly remembering the baby in the well dream. He'd had that dream when he was forty-three.

"It's hard to find a new job when you're in your forties. How old are you?"

"What?" said Joshua. "Why do you want to know?"

Harmony shrugged. "No reason." Her mind was racing—racing too fast with her own thoughts to hear any of his—but her newly trained diaphragm was deep breathing without effort. Suddenly, she was noticing things: She noticed that Joshua didn't tell her his age. She noticed that it didn't even occur to him to tell her. It didn't occur to him to say, "Yeah, I know how hard it can be when you think you're supposed to have it all together and it all falls apart. I know because I'm in trouble too. My wife left me and I'm afraid I'll never be Superman." Harmony noticed that her heart was breaking for all the things Joshua didn't think to, or couldn't, say, and suddenly, she couldn't stand one more minute of not saying—out loud—what was important. She couldn't bear staying the same. Alone. And suddenly she remembered the baby in the well dream and how she'd given Delilah to Joshua, and he hadn't said thank you. No matter how scary it was to say things, it was scarier not to.

"You want to know something personal about me?" she blurted. "I really like Hillary Rodham Clinton. I voted for her for Senator. How about you?"

Joshua shifted from one foot to the other and decided to keep it light. "I was fond of Bill." Harmony turned to gather her things from the corner against the wall. "Okay, okay, I voted for her too," he said, smiling.

Psychopaths control through seduction, remembered Harmony, but she about-faced anyway. "Sometimes I think I look like Hillary. Only shorter.

And darker. I would have known Bill was lying. I always know. I know things in my body," she said, looking at him hard. Joshua looked blank. "I'm telling you something personal."

"That's good," said Joshua, confused. Why was he stuck on the baby in the well dream? It was running around his head in a loop.

"You said the only way to change is to know our own greatness. That's my greatness—I know things in my body; I'm a knower. How about you?"

Joshua wasn't used to feeling uncomfortable with his students. "Sure," he said, "I know things."

"I know you," said Harmony purposefully. If she waited one more second, she would never say it. And if she never said it, she would never change. She would die in inexorable disconnection, a half-person, neither here nor there. "I not only know you, I love you." Her face burned and she felt like her heart was going to explode out of her chest, but it kept beating—as her feet shot roots down six floors, through the thick New York City concrete, into the center of the earth. "Thank you," she said. "Thank you."

Joshua couldn't speak. And if he could have, he wouldn't. Harmony knew this in one devastating moment of clarity. And that was that.

"Well, I guess I should get going," she said. "I have to go home and get some sleep because tomorrow is another day of unemployment." And they both laughed.

Chapter 39

CAROUSEL

At the end of August, Grace called to say that Quentin had left the conglomerate and was starting a new magazine for "cultural creatives," the growing market of people who made decisions based on their souls' needs rather than conventional concerns. Quentin was going to act as both publisher and editor for the first issue, and Grace was putting together a staff. They couldn't offer benefits yet, but would Harmony like to do some part-time work managing and maybe write some articles, and before Grace had even mentioned money, Harmony was yelling, "Yes!"

"Cut it with the grain," she commanded the baffled hair stylist when she went for her first professional haircut since Delilah's death. "And how much do manicures cost?" She wanted to look extra nice for her first day at the first job with the first people she really wanted to be with.

The office was a couple of windowless rooms sublet in a sprawling financial firm founded by one of Quentin's oldest and dearest friends, and space was tight. But Harmony was so thrilled to be writing stories that she didn't care. And when Grace said she needed a good bookkeeper, Harmony recommended Ruth. Finally, finally, the perfect family.

Quentin even allowed music in the office. He preferred jazz. Grace brought Bach's cello suites. Ruth brought blues. And even though it embarrassed her to expose her penchant for Broadway show music, Harmony brought *Carousel*. They took turns. Everybody got a day to play their own music.

Grace felt a little guilty for not inviting Cora and started to explain that they were too small to need a secretary, but Harmony gestured that she didn't have to hear this, and Grace smiled. They both knew that Cora wouldn't bring the right understanding to a magazine called *Aware Choices*.

But Harmony, who didn't usually miss people, felt a sweet pang in her heart at the mention of Cora's name. Then she remembered Dr. T's comment about how when you saw someone it could make you cry. And the thought of Dr. T made her feel like crying. What on earth was happening? And in her big mind, she heard Dr. T say, "You're being human. Welcome to the world."

At Grace's recommendation, Harmony pitched Quentin some feature stories on socially responsible intuitive investing, houseplants that heal, and dealing with your over-sensitive nature. Quentin chose the sensitivity piece.

Even though it made her miss Delilah, Harmony took the bus to 72nd Street. She walked west to Central Park and strolled with her pad and pen to the Ramble. Sometimes she craved quiet and birds and trees the way you can crave a food. She made herself comfortable on one of her favorite benches looking out over the lake and Bethesda Fountain on the other side, and she drafted the sensitivity piece.

> Do people tell you you're hyper-sensitive? Do you get overwhelmed by your emotions? Do you wish you could turn it all off?
>
> Well, maybe the solution is not turning off, but instead tuning in to what you're feeling. Did you know that emotions have smells? Energetic impact? Temperature? By noticing the specifics of what you sense, you can begin to learn the language of subtle information and better understand the unspoken realities of your experiences.
>
> For instance, you are in a business meeting. You put forth an idea and suddenly you notice a smell like mildew coming from your boss—

Quentin put down the draft and looked at Harmony. "Where did you get this?"

He really did look like Superman and Harmony sometimes had trouble not staring at him. Also, it was her show music day and, since it was only 8:30 and the finance people were still having coffee, "The Carousel Waltz" was on full-volume which made Harmony long to dance and glide. "I'm sorry. What did you say?"

"I asked where you got this material," said Quentin. "What was your research?"

Oh god. In her excitement about writing stories, she never even contemplated this most obvious question. "Well," she began. She coughed a couple of times and blushed.

"Look," said Quentin. His eyes were kind. "It doesn't matter. The writing is fine, but we can't publish anything without credible research. We need to establish ourselves—particularly in this first issue—as a voice of authority. We're walking a fine line between hard-core service and, although I never want this term associated with us, New Age. We're writing about what everybody knows in their gut, but we have to prove it with credible research. People are afraid to believe what they know. *Capiche*?"

Harmony stared at her lap. "Of course. I'm an idiot. Sorry."

"Hey," said Quentin, "none of that."

Harmony looked up, and the expression in his eyes made her wish he weren't gay. How on earth did a man like this have sex with Joseph Timiani?

"You judge too harshly," said Quentin, and Harmony gulped air. "Let me show you something," said Quentin, getting up suddenly. "Grace," he called, "let's show Harmony the view. And, Ruth, you, too."

Harmony fancied herself a perceptive person. How had she managed to work at *Your Garden* for five years without noticing that Quentin was a saint? She realized this as she followed him out to the financial office's trading room with windows on two sides. All she'd seen was her tiny cubicle of discontent. She'd never even wondered about the rest of the people at the company.

"Just look at this," said Quentin, motioning for Harmony, Ruth, and Grace to join him at the window.

"It's spectacular!" sighed Grace, and a couple of the finance men gave her the once-over as they sipped coffee. Harmony noticed how comfortable Grace was. She simply smiled at being appreciated.

"Sometimes it takes a bird's-eye view for things to make sense," said Quentin. They were so high in the sky that the cars looked like toys and the people mere specks—all moving in an immaculate order. Across the street, the trees in the little cemetery behind St. Paul's Chapel looked like a patch of forest in an H.O. train set scene. The sky was clear and blue. "The

Carousel Waltz" made the perfect music score behind such a pristine vista. "You don't mind the music, do you guys?" said Quentin to the brokers, but before they could answer: "Too bad if you do. You need some cultcha!" And everyone laughed.

"Tomorrow I'll bring in *Brigadoon*," said Harmony.

"Tomorrow is Billie Holiday!" declared Ruth, elbowing Harmony in the ribs. "God, I wish my Billy could see this. He always wanted to be up in the sky. . . . But then, again, maybe he is."

And it was with that exact thought, in that exact moment, that Harmony suddenly felt a sweetness in her chest so powerful that it broke her own heart. Her eyes got hot with tears and she blinked hard, afraid if anyone saw they'd think she was nuts. But just at that moment, Quentin laid his warm hand on her shoulder as if to say "What in the world could ever be wrong?" and she stopped worrying and let one fat tear pool and drop out of her eye. And her chest swelled with the sweetness, and she couldn't see straight with all that heat and tears, and now the pain in her heart was cracking it wide open, and she *really* couldn't see—it was as if she and Ruth and Grace and Quentin and the room itself suddenly faded so that what normally appeared real looked ghostly, fuzzy—swirling as a kind of light reflection from something too big, too blindingly bright to describe. Harmony felt the source of the reflection like a pulsation of something bigger than a million trillion suns, and the room filled with the intoxicating smell of gardenias. Could it be coming from her heart, or her breasts which suddenly felt mammoth, or maybe somewhere else? Outside and inside were meaningless concepts. And suddenly she realized there was absolutely nothing to worry about or hide, and she let the tears run because she knew unequivocally that nothing was or had ever been bad. Life was just a funny play of swirling, twirling reflections, and Quentin's hand on her shoulder felt so soothing. And for no reason in particular, she hooked arms with Grace on one side and Ruth on the other, and she stuck out her big breasts which suddenly felt perfect—the perfect size to nurse the world.

"The paradox," continued Quentin on his previous train of thought, "is that in order to get a bird's-eye view, you have to be rooted. And you can't be really rooted unless you're willing to let other people—"

And that's when they heard the roar, saw the plane, felt death. They were facing east, but they saw the pilot's granite face as the north windows exploded and the world blew up—air on fire, screams drowned by roar, the end.

"JUMP!" yelled Quentin, diving head-first like Superman as the building disintegrated.

"NOW!" commanded that guardian voice that had always been there. And bucking the impulse to "Hug" into a safe ball, Harmony opened her heart and jumped. All three women did. With "The Carousel Waltz" in their hearts drowning the roar in their heads, they fell ninety-five floors. They never let go of each other. They fell like fiery angels linked arm-in-arm, disappearing into nothing on impact.

EPILOGUE

September classes were canceled due to the World Trade Center disaster. Joshua told Martha to call everyone, and he disappeared. And even though Martha was now living with Joshua, he didn't tell her where he was going.

When he returned in October, he looked thin. Deflated. Martha was concerned, but Joshua assured her he was fine, and of course he knew best.

Dr. Thompson heard the news and knew immediately that Harmony was gone. In her last session she'd been so happy about her new job up in the clouds with people she liked. She'd told Dr. Thompson about the last exchange with Joshua and said she was at peace.

On an impulse, Dr. Thompson looked up the school's phone number. She knew about the voice mail system from Harmony's furious story about the unreturned message, so she was surprised when Joshua picked up.

"Hello?" he said. "This is the Healing School."

"Hello," said Dr. Thompson. "My name is Estelle Thompson." She paused, but Joshua was silent. "Is this Joshua?" she asked.

"Yes," he answered.

"I don't know if Harmony Rogers ever mentioned my name. I'm her therapist."

"Yes," said Joshua and waited.

"She didn't have any family, and I didn't know who else to call."

"Yes," said Joshua.

This was not going to be easy. "She had started a new job in the World Trade Center."

"Yes," said Joshua. "With one of my other students, Grace Dominick. We're all devastated."

"Oh," said Dr. Thompson. The sudden confirmation took her breath away. "I'm sorry," she said, her voice breaking.

"It's all right," said Joshua.

His tone was soft, and Dr. Thompson felt the gentleness that Harmony had described. "I know she had a very special relationship with you."

"Harmony was very sensitive. But as we both probably know, she was prone to . . ."—he tried to find the right words—"flights of fantasy."

Dr. Thompson was quiet. "She had a feeling for you. And I must say I'm personally grateful for whatever you did."

"Well, I thank you," said Joshua. "I can only imagine what she told you. But if believing in her projections helped her, I'm glad."

Dr. Thompson swallowed. "I'm not exactly sure what to do now—about her apartment. Arrangements. There really is nobody else to take care of things. I could use some assistance. I'm sure the super would let us in."

Joshua agreed to meet Dr. Thompson at Harmony's apartment, and together they would try to sort things out. Dr. Thompson thanked him profusely as she didn't want to do this alone, and Joshua said it was his honor to help.

On a good day, Dr. Thompson had no sense of direction and was not fond of subways, but this was not a good day. She almost never went to the Lower Eastside, and not only did she take the wrong train and end up at Eighth Street and Astor Place, but she was so disoriented on exiting that she walked east instead of south. The mayor had only recently lifted the downtown blockade, and even though there was no obvious damage, the neighborhood felt foreign and smelled like a war zone. The air was so thick with acridity that Dr. Thompson covered her face with her scarf and tried to breathe through her mouth. The filth coated everything, including street signs, so it wasn't until she hit Avenue B that she realized her mistake and headed south . . . past the community garden. "Oh!" she moaned seeing the broken plants and dead tree limbs—a killing field covered in the acrid filth. Her eyes burned, and she fished through her purse for sunglasses.

By the time she got to the building on Broome Street, her eyes were streaming and she wished she had thought to wear waterproof mascara.

"Hi," said Joshua.

"Hi," said Dr. Thompson. "I hope I didn't keep you waiting too long." She removed her glasses and wiped at her face with the scarf. "I'm probably a mess."

"Don't worry about it," said Joshua, barely looking at her. "The super gave me the keys."

The first thing they noticed in Harmony's apartment was the plants. The second things only Joshua saw: A ghostly being hovering above the living room windows; it disappeared as they entered. And a cockroach in a dark corner in front of an enormous wood-framed mirror that reflected it, making it look like two big bugs. It stared impudently at Joshua, then skittered into a crack in the floorboards.

"She told me she liked houseplants, but I had no idea," gasped Dr. Thompson. The place was a joyful jungle, a refuge from the devastation of the streets—complete with what looked like a complicated air filtration and now-empty humidifying system; it was the first time since landing on Eighth Street that Dr. Thompson could breathe. This indoor oasis was completed with a waterless water garden whose pump was making a death rattle from gulping air. Dr. Thompson went into the bedroom and unplugged it. She stared at the tiny toy animals arranged in pairs on the rocks. They looked as if they were kissing. Dr. Thompson touched her heart.

"Dr. Thompson," called Joshua.

Something about the formality startled her. "Please, call me Estelle," she said, walking out to the living room.

Joshua stared blankly.

"Estelle," she repeated.

"Estelle," said Joshua. He hadn't spoken that name since his mother died.

"My father was a stargazer," she offered—trying to lighten the mood. "Estelle. It means star."

"Oh," said Joshua, busying himself looking at the plants. "That's nice. I was just noticing these are bone dry, but nothing's dead." And he quashed an impulse to run by cupping his hand around an outrageously large—almost obscene—fire-engine red geranium blossom. Then he examined the orange buds pushing up through the cleavage of strappy green *clivia* leaves; the strands of wandering Jew draped between windows, royal purple on the underside, iridescent silver striped on the other where the sun's light reflected; and finally a pot of dirt. He picked it up, and on closer examination, saw a bunch of cylindrical green clumps pushing up around the perimeter. "That's a snake plant," said Dr. Thompson, startling him.

"Oh," said Joshua, holding it tighter. He suddenly felt so tired, he was afraid he might drop it. "I really don't know anything about plants. I'm a city boy. I gotta sit down."

"*Sanseveria* is its proper name," said Dr. T, feeling equally exhausted. "She told me about it."

"You have a good memory," said Joshua, collapsing into the couch cradling the pot of dirt and buds.

"Mind if I join you?" said Dr. T, not waiting for his reply.

And they sat there—Dr. T ignoring her sudden impulse to hold Joshua's hand and Joshua pretending he didn't long to lay his head in Estelle Thompson's massive warm lap.

"So what did she tell you about the plant?" said Joshua when he could no longer stand the silence.

"She rescued it from somebody's garbage," answered Dr. T. "Then it got damaged at work. It looked dead, she said, but she brought it home anyway because snake plants are nearly indestructible. She never gave up on her 'rescuees,' as she called them. She said it would come back She didn't believe in death."

"I guess she was right," said Joshua, fingering the leaf clumps. "Listen, I wonder if you can help me with something. I'm sure Harmony told you—"

"I can't help you with anything," interrupted Dr. T. "I really can't help anybody with anything. All I ever do is listen."

Joshua stuck his pointer finger in the dry dirt, then pulled it out. "Me too," he said. "I didn't mean to—"

Dr. T silenced him with a gesture, and they both understood the sometimes loneliness of the confidentiality of their professions.

Joshua fingered the buds in the pot of dirt. Dr. T admired the gentleness of Joshua's touch on the new growth. She was so glad Harmony had found him. "Why don't you take that home with you?" she said. "I'm sure Harmony would want you to have it."

"You think?" said Joshua, raising the pot to eye level. It was very heavy and he felt so tired—too tired to feel afraid of the deflatedness in his chest, too tired to pretend he didn't feel tired, too tired to run away from Estelle Thompson by asking deflective questions. "Do you really think I should take this?"

"Yes, I do," said Dr. Thompson. "I most certainly do."

"I can't help anybody with anything either," he said, letting the pot drop to his lap.

"You know the most interesting thing she told me about that plant?" said Dr. T. Joshua shook his head. "It's the only houseplant that produces oxygen at night—in the dark. All the others do it in the daytime. It thrives in the dark."

"Very interesting," said Joshua politely, cradling the heavy stoneware pot and wondering what the hell he was about to do.

"Maybe it will help," said Dr. T.

Joshua considered this and didn't say "Help what?" or "I don't need help" or "I'm here to help you and I have no fear of the dark." Instead, for no reason in particular, he hooked arms with Estelle Thompson, and Estelle, the stargazer's daughter, didn't analyze or intellectualize or wonder about his psychotherapeutic credentials, but she returned the gesture by squeezing his arm into the side of her big soft breast. And it was at that exact moment that both of them felt a sweetness so powerful that it broke open their hearts. Their eyes got hot with tears, but neither of them cried. Instead, Estelle Thompson pointed to the snake plant pot in Joshua Gardner's lap and said, "Take it home."

"Home!" ordered a voice that only Joshua heard.

"Okay then," said Joshua. "Home it goes." Then he smiled at Estelle, and although he didn't say it, Estelle heard his thoughts:

"Thank you. Thank you. Thank you."

And the room filled with the light of fiery angels, and had there been music, it would have been "The Carousel Waltz."

ABOUT THE AUTHOR

Betsy Robinson writes funny fiction about flawed people. Her novel *The Last Will & Testament of Zelda McFigg* is winner of Black Lawrence Press's 2013 Big Moose Prize and was published in September 2014. This was followed by the February 2015 publication of her edit of *The Trouble with the Truth* by Edna Robinson, Betsy's late mother, by Simon & Schuster/Infinite Words. She published revised e-book and paperback editions of her Mid-List Press award-winning first novel, a tragicomedy about falling down the rabbit hole of the U.S. of A. in the 1970s, *Plan Z by Leslie Kove*, when it went out of print. Her articles have been published in *Publishers Weekly*, Lithub, *Chicago Review of Books*, *Oh Reader*, *The Sunlight Press*, *Prairie Fire*, Salvation South, Next Avenue, and many other publications. Betsy is an editor, fiction writer, journalist, and playwright. Her website is www.BetsyRobinson-writer.com.

ABOUT KANO PRESS

Kano Press takes its name from the oracle rune Kano, which stands for Opening, Fire, Torch. A rune is a letter in a runic alphabet used to write Germanic languages before the Latin alphabet was adopted. The symbol for kano is <, or reversed >. Runes inscribed on small stone pieces that are blindly drawn from a bag are used to aid our understanding of whatever issue we choose or to provide guidance. Drawing < signifies opening and renewed clarity, freedom to both receive gifts and to know the joy of nonattached giving. If one draws the reversed position, >, it signifies a darkening of the light and advises to give up the old, live on empty, develop inner stability, and wait for illumination.

Three guiding quotations:

> "I mean, if you have any idea of any kind of complexity or immensity or destiny, of general order, you're put in a position of nothingness. And I think this is true. I don't think I'm anything; I never have thought that. Whatever it is that activates it is a certain kind of energy that goes on. But the effect is ridiculous; it's absurd."
>
> —Lincoln Kirstein in *The New Yorker*

> "When I see heavy dramas with no comic relief, I don't think they're honest. I don't think people go through life miserable all the time; in fact, if you're very miserable, you giggle a lot at the oddest things."
>
> —Carl Reiner in *The Trib*

"In the same way that . . . the listener completes the song, I believe if you give them a certain sound and you place it just far enough so that they can just hear it, it creates a depth in your hearing and that depth, just like if you imagine the church bells in the distance, there's something about that that opens the listener . . . there's something about these distant sounds that open us up emotionally and if as a writer, a songwriter, I can produce sounds that allow the listener to open themselves emotionally, then whatever I have to say lyrically has a chance of being really meaningful."

—Paul Simon, "Smartless" podcast

Kano Press aspires to publish books that include humor and a transcendent point of view, stories that evoke openings.

Other Books by Betsy Robinson

The Spectators (coming in 2024)
Lily Hogue, a reluctant psychic, joins with a band of loner women to deal with the true nature of time, destruction, loss, and love.

Plan Z by Leslie Kove
A funny and poignant novel about negotiating life without a plan, without a clue. With PTSD.

Girl Stories & Game Plays
24 stories and 3 one-act plays—a feast of silly, serious, strange, sexy, transcendent, and laugh-out-loud funny stories and plays with playable scenes

The Last Will & Testament of Zelda McFigg
A raucously funny novel about doing whatever is necessary to survive. Winner of Black Lawrence Press's Big Moose Prize

The Trouble with the Truth
An actor's sister's story of growing up in the shadow of her dramatic brother in the 1930s and '40s. (Edited by Betsy, written by her late mother, Edna.)

Conversations with Mom: An Aging Baby Boomer, in Need of an Elder, Writes to Her Dead Mother
A funny and moving little book for anyone who's struggled with being human.

COMING IN FALL 2024

From Kano Press

PREVIEW EXCERPT

THE SPECTATORS

By Betsy Robinson

CHAPTER 1

I came late. I was not there at the start of the event. Yet I can envision the details as though I were. It is a Monday in early January of 2017. A partly sunny afternoon in New York City. Thirty-seven degrees. High humidity, maybe a drizzle on the way. The view up Broadway is overcast. The two relatively new high-rises on either side of West Seventy-second Street are muted in the fog, ugly against the gray sky, and the old-world, tiered wedding-cake beauty of the Ansonia Hotel just north on Seventy-fourth almost apologizes for them. A small flock of gray pigeons soars in counterclockwise circles from the east side of Amsterdam Avenue over the CapitalOne Bank, climbing in altitude west over the landmarked Central Savings building, spreading and diving southwest, then compacting into a tight clump of silver slivers as the sun hits their bodies through a brief break in the clouds over the islands of Verdi Square and the Seventy-second Street IRT subway station. Morning rush hour is long over and it will be more than an hour till the streets clog with neighborhood residents pouring out of the station in exhausted yet impatient herds. The traffic light at the fork where Broadway splits into upper Broadway and Amsterdam is yellow when the white van with the "Trump for President" sticker rear-ends the bug-like Smartcar, throwing it onto its side as the van's driver careens left, through the guardrail and into the subway station. Some freeze, others dive; bodies fly, bones crack. A horrible accident! A man in a hardhat working on a scaffold above the Tasty Café on Seventy-first vaults to the street and runs to help. Women scream. Babies shriek. What a crazy driver! Call 9-1-1! yells the hardhat. People on cell phones turn them to record as bodies are dragged out from under the van.

The driver. Check the driver!

A wide-bodied, middle-aged Black woman in a cheap wool coat over violet scrubs hurtles a fragile white woman in a wheelchair across the street away from the accident and parks her next to the benches on Verdi Square. "I've heard these benches have bedbugs," says the white woman haughtily, eying a crow perched on the bench back; odd that he didn't fly off at the crash.

"Wait for me," answers the Black woman, and then she waddles as fast as her weight will allow back across the street, and that's when the van blows up.

Lily Hogue, the discomfited woman in the wheelchair, tracks the upsurge and scattering of pigeons at the sound of an explosion as the van bursts into flame. She forgot her eyeglasses in the restaurant, but if she tries very hard, if she squints so tightly that her sea-blue eyes tear, as if viewing in her mind's eye a play being played through a scrim by the tiny people fleeing the scene, if she breathes low into her sagging belly, she can remember as clearly as I see this day that she was once a member of the scurry. Although she was born with her mother's thick, flaxen hair, good bone structure, and, eventually, the long, leggy gams of a super model, now her hair is so wispy and white that, when sunlit, it's merely translucent fluff, exposing Lily as a pink-scalped head atop a bone-thin face with crinkled paper-like skin; she has not aged well due to the recent stress. But considering the alternative, the fact that she *has* aged certainly is a coup. Lily is a month shy of sixty-six—old for a family where everybody died young—wars, suicides, accidents, three killed at one time by falling off a mountaintop, several murders, and at least one electrocution by lightning. Her longevity is due to good luck and the fact that she has not been particularly adventuresome. Until today.

Her attendant is clearly dead. Lily knows this from the sound and the heat that is radiating from the other side of the street. She supposes that getting back to the restaurant to retrieve her eyeglasses is no longer an option. She wonders if Medicare will pay for a second eye exam in one year. There must be a record of the prescription somewhere, but for the life of her, she can't remember where, and Nanette, her attendant, took care of those things.

People are rushing across Amsterdam Avenue to the island of Verdi Square to gawk. As the south end of the square fills, Lily, panting and pushing, laboriously edges her chair toward the north end, far enough from the action not to be singed by the heat, but close enough to feel the air burst when the second explosion comes and the crow finally takes off. At the blast, she is overwhelmed by déjà vu and painfully aware that this is no accident, and she remembers all that is to follow.

There are never any accidents. I know that now that I have watched this whole story play out. Only cycles and patterns—patterns of movement, patterns of events, patterns of attractions and aversions. Right now, for instance, in the present scene, there is an avid throng of onlookers at the south end of the square. Some are crying, others are trying to push to the front, certain that they can help or at least be part of the action because they are People Who Act. In front of them, in the street, several police officers who appeared out of who-knows-where are bellowing orders. Sirens wail from south on Amsterdam where the fire station has stopped traffic and dispatched every truck on the premises. As the crowd balloons, they expand toward the north end of the square. There is a group of teenagers screaming and laughing hysterically, not because they are amused, but because they must release their explosive adolescent energy, their response to the tragedy. Near the front are two girls, maybe fifteen, and Lily feels a familiarity as she watches their dance: One is sparkly-eyed and sure of herself as she points, directing her friend to take a photo of her and to make certain she gets a good angle so it's clear that sparkle-eyes is part of what will no doubt be a historic act of terrorism on the six o'clock news. Maybe they can even get their video on TV. The girl with the cell phone camera wears a pale yellow parka with a fur-fringed hood. "Cathy, now!" yells sparkle-eyes. "What's the matter with you?" Sparkle-eyes has perfectly symmetrical features, a sharp little nose, and short brown hair curled back to expose gold hoop earrings. "Cathy!"

But Cathy is frozen. Useless.

See Kano Press for Updates

betsyrobinson-writer.com/KanoPress.com.htm